W9-BIM-404

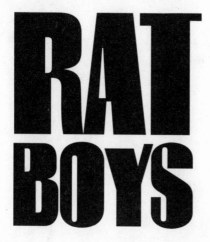

RAT BOYS

*A Dating
Experiment*

by **THOM EBERHARDT**

Hyperion
New York

Copyright © 2001 by Thom Eberhardt

All rights reserved. No part of this book may be reproduced or transmitted in any form or by any means, electronic or mechanical, including photocopying, recording, or by any information storage and retrieval system, without written permission from the publisher. For information address Hyperion Books for Children, 114 Fifth Avenue, New York, New York 10011-5690.
First Edition
1 3 5 7 9 10 8 6 4 2

Printed in the United States of America
This book is set in 9.5-point Leawood Book

Library of Congress Cataloging-in-Publication Data
Eberhardt, Thom.
Rat Boys / by Thom Eberhardt.—1st ed.
    p.   cm.
Summary: Fourteen-year-olds Marci and Summer use a magic ring to turn two rats into cute boys so that they can have dates for the Spring Fling.
ISBN 0-7868-0696-6 (trade)
[1. Magic—Fiction. 2. Rats—Fiction. 3. Humorous stories.]
I. Title.

PZ7.E175 Rat 2001
[Fic]—dc21   2001016630
Visit www.hyperionchildrensbooks.com

To my daughters, Dana and Kate,
who loaned me their voices

Foreword

$\mathcal{M}$y name is Marci Kornbalm. My best friend since preschool is Summer Weingarten. This story happened to Summer and me on March 22 of last year when we were in the second half of the ninth grade. We were fourteen and facing humiliation beyond belief, which I freely admit was my fault (and did at the time, too).

This story also happened to a few other people besides us, particularly Doris Trowbridge. Doris is around forty years old or something, has astigmatism and a very serious overbite. She also tends to be a bit overweight due to antirejection medication and is usually called "Weird Doris" by other people.

I should probably tell you that there is a magic ring in this story. But before you go, *"Magic ring?! Give me a break!"* and put this up on the shelf, behind that old copy of *Heidi,* I want you to know that the ring is hardly in the story at all.

This whole thing is really about the first dates Summer and I ever had in our lives, which were these two totally cool, cute-beyond-belief guys. I am not kidding about this—they were to drool and die for.

So, forget the magic ring aspect if you want and just concentrate on the guy aspect. That's exactly what we did last March 22.

Summer and Me

So like I said, Summer Weingarten has been my very best friend since forever. We live in Glenwood, Indiana. It's south of Indianapolis off of I-70. There's a Circle K at the off-ramp with a sign that's way bigger than the sign that says GLENWOOD WELCOMES YOU.

It used to be this little town from about a hundred years ago, but now it's mostly tract homes full of people who work in Indianapolis. The old-town part is still there, but they built a mall and that's where everyone goes to buy stuff, usually. The old part of town has mostly lawn mower repair guys and stuff like that.

Doris Trowbridge has a shop in the old-town part. It's called Hidden Treasures. WE BUY JUNK, WE SELL ANTIQUES is written on the window, but I have absolutely no idea who the "we" is, because Doris owns it and she's all by herself, an aspect of this story that is going to be pretty important later on.

Just down and across the street from her shop is Herb Is Handy, which belongs to Herb the handyman. He's, like, this guy that comes to your house and gets forks out of your garbage disposal when they slip down it and make it jam. He drives around in this old pickup that's got HERB IS HANDY written on it. How embarrassing is that? Welcome to my world.

Just imagine the most boring place you've ever been. No. Imagine a place so boring, you can't even imagine it. It's so boring, *I* can't even imagine it and I live there. In fact, my mom and dad also come from Glenwood, and my grandparents on both sides are from around here. We're pretty boring people.

Summer's family is more diverse, but not much more. Her mom grew up in Glenwood and went to high school with my parents. She met Summer's dad in Texas, where she happened to be four times a day, being a flight attendant for Big Horizon Airlines (which mostly flies back and forth between Chicago and Dallas). Summer's dad is this chemist guy and had this really good job doing chemistry in Texas. Then he gets transferred from Texas back to Indianapolis. So what happens? They buy a house in Glenwood. How Twilight Zone is that? It's, like, you can't escape.

Summer's memory of the world outside of Glenwood and surrounding towns (such as Maplewood, Oakwood, and probably Plywood) is sadly fuzzy, because all this moving happened when she was very little. At least she has pictures.

Besides my mom and dad, I have this older sister who is currently at Nevada State. When she graduated from high school she wanted to go to college as far away from Glenwood as we could afford, and Nevada was it. I encouraged her to go as much as I could on account of how much we fight about stuff. She was an only child for a really long time, then I came along and wrecked it for her. My parents called me "Mom's big surprise." My sister called me other things. From the time she was seven (when I happened) to the time she was thirteen, she had this whole major chip on her shoulder over it. After that, it got a little better between her and me. Still, I wasn't that upset to see her go. I got her room.

Summer has no sisters or brothers but has some cousins. She's got this particularly cute one who went into the army or air force or something, whose name is Steve. He's not in this story at all, but some of his clothes are (he always has these really cool clothes all the time).

Summer and I met when our mothers enrolled us in Miss Vicky's Dance Class. Those were really great days because, for one thing, everyone always used to say how cute we were since I'm sort of dark, with brown curly hair, and Summer is this total blonde. People used to call us "Salt and Pepper" (I was the pepper, Summer was the salt). I guess we hit it off from the start, because my mom has all these pictures of us and we're always holding hands when we went places and dancing next to each other and everything.

We used to be the same size once, but that all changed in the last two years. It's like this destiny thing. I have these short, curly-haired genes and she has these tall blond flight-attendant genes.

Between fifth and sixth grade, Summer started to seriously chub out. My mom warned me not to make comments about it, but it was hard to avoid the subject. I mean, there I was, still pretty much the same as always, and Summer was oozing out of everything. It was the last year that either of us had bathing suits with Minnie Mouse or any other cartoon character on them (Summer's was actually Bubbles from the Power Puff Girls). I remember that Summer's bathing suit kept riding up and the elastic would dig into her thighs and leave marks, and I felt so bad about it. By the end of that summer, she started always wearing a T-shirt over her bathing suit and I never saw her any other way.

Her seventh-grade school ID picture was a disaster. Not only had she chubbed out, but the camera flash was too close to her, which blondes in particular have to watch out for, and she came out looking like a meringue pie with ears and eyeballs. Also, her mother got her this perm that was supposed to be a new-look thing to help her self-image. But they went to this beautician who just got out of rehab (we found out later) and wasn't too good with perms. So besides looking like a meringue pie, she also looked like she stuck her tongue in a lightbulb socket. This was sort of a low point for Summer.

It turned out that her chubbiness was actually part of what I call the "accordion effect." It's almost like that old joke, "I don't need to lose weight; I need to grow four inches." And Summer did, accordioning out.

Now she has these long legs and enough of a figure to

look great in various stretch tops, but not so much that she has to worry about major saggies later in life.

Me? I had just the opposite problem. All through middle school, when everybody was getting into two-piece bathing suits and starting to look okay in them, I was known as "the girl with two backs." And about the most I can say for my legs, even now, is that they touch the ground.

These days Summer and I think we look okay and mostly have what I consider to be good self-esteem. It's not that we think we're perfect, because we don't. I have this kind of too big nose and she has ears that stick out. But it's not like we don't live in modern times. Right?

Those things that are wrong with us we figure can be surgically altered later on as required (which includes figure enhancement for me if it's not happening to my satisfaction by the time I graduate). This is not to say that we always had such good self-esteem or such total faith in laser technology. Last year was such a different story altogether, I can't even believe it.

Summer had not yet fully adjusted to her growth spurt and thus, not fully regaining her coordination, was bumping into things pretty regularly (it was four inches in thirteen months, for crying out loud!). So she would trip over curbs, smack into doors, get hit with various soccer balls, softballs, and tennis balls, and was kind of banged up on any given day.

Our cycles were also synchronized, which is this weird girl thing that happens when you're really close to someone, like we are with each other. This meant that we were depressed and/or pissed off for the same couple of days every month, which made it hard to for us cheer each other up at those times (though we could always count on each other for Midol when needed).

We were also fully involved with the orthodontist at about the same time. I got uppers, and Summer got uppers and lowers. Her dad is significantly taller than her mother, which accounts for the added problems in jaw alignment.

That year we were getting our bands tightened on the first and third Fridays of every month and, because of our cycles, one or the other of the visits was probably going to be very annoying and/or depressing. And, like, even if you're not all doubled over with cramps or crying your eyes out over self-esteem issues, an orthodontist can still wreck your whole day, either through major guilt trips about not flossing and gum massaging properly or through substantial physical pain.

Here's a question: Why do dentists and orthodontists put those gross scary pictures all over their walls? Those closeup shots, blown up to about ten times their normal size, of mouths that are so ugly and rotten that it's hard to believe they're for real. Think about it. If someone actually had teeth like that, would they allow pictures to be taken and then posted for everyone to look at all the time? I'm really sure.

No, it's my theory that these pictures are there as this total threat. So, no matter how bad the pain is and how much you suddenly think your teeth aren't that bad and that a slight gap can be kind of sexy anyway, those pictures are there to keep you coming back again and again, especially if you have a good dental plan.

This particular visit was on March 22 of last year, except

it was in the morning instead of the afternoon because we didn't have school. It was Spring Fling weekend.

Spring Fling is this big carnival kind of thing that Glenwood has every year. There are all kinds of rides and booths with locally grown produce and school projects that teachers set up so parents will think their kids might get into a good college (which is why we have Friday off, because the teachers are setting up). There is also this big dance that kicks the whole thing off. Not with just a DJ, but usually with a band.

You have to be at least twelve to get into the dance part of it unless accompanied by a parent (as if!). So Summer and I started practicing our dancing when we were ten, even though we had two years to go. We don't like to put things off until the last minute.

We would go to the Kickapoo Pavilion (which is at the fairgrounds and where the dance goes on) and watch from the door to see how good we had to be. You have to look past the parents who are trying to dance so you can see the high school kids. There really needs to be some sensitivity training for parents and various older types in this regard. If you are somebody's parent or over thirty, do not attempt dancing to music written in the modern era. You won't be able to do it, and you run the risk of humiliating those related to you.

After watching the high school kids, we would practice in front of various mirrors. By the sixth grade, we were confident enough to practice in the front yard, using the stereo from Summer's mom's Voyager when it was parked in the carport. Besides having really good bass, it's got tinted windows, so we could also watch our reflections.

By the seventh grade we were inside the dance. We stood against the wall, bouncing to the music in a way that sort of told everybody that we could dance without causing embarrassment to anyone who might ask us. Nobody did.

Summer was convinced that it was because of her ID picture and suggested that I stand some distance away from her. Of course I didn't. Secretly, I thought our not getting asked by anybody was just as likely to have something to do with my nose.

Another year of practice and we were ready again. By this time Summer had started her growth spurt and, though neither of us said anything, we were each concerned about her lack of coordination. Without acknowledging the reason, we agreed to confine ourselves to slow dances.

Rod & Tod were both there, which was an early indication of how the night might go. They are twins and in our same class at school. Once upon a time they were kind of cute. That was back when their mother dressed them and checked them over real good before they were allowed out in public. Despite her efforts, Rod & Tod had succumbed to bad grooming and obnoxious behavior as they got older. So, not only were we not being asked to dance at all (slow or otherwise), but we were also being stalked by Rod & Tod.

Lucky for us, we had heard them bragging about winning a whoopee cushion after playing Skeeball for three hours, so we, like, knew the deal. The rest of the night was spent keeping away from them and trying to look available to dance at the same time. How impossible is that?

So there we were, on the morning of our third Spring

Fling dance, face-to-face with giant pictures of rotting teeth and another year of standing against the wall for three hours. As if that wasn't enough, Summer carried an extra burden.

Remember how I told you that Summer's dad was this chemist guy? It turns out that he invented this new improved formula for artificial saliva and (wouldn't you just know it) had to pick the day before the Spring Fling to announce that it had been approved by the FDA.

"FRESHMAN'S DAD CURES DRY MOUTH" was the caption in the school paper right under Summer's picture—the only time she has ever been in the school paper. Yikes!

By the way, if you think there's no such thing as artificial saliva, go to any drugstore and ask. I did when I first heard about it, because I was all, like, "Get out of here!" But there it was.

I bring this up for two reasons. First, to show the kind of things that happen to Summer and me on a daily basis and especially at those times when we would prefer not to be humiliated.

Second is to make this point about life in general. As you read this story, things are going to get very weird. And maybe you'll be, like, "I'm so sure that would happen." But just remember one thing, okay? Anything is possible in a world where people pay money for fake spit.

Future Truth

*J*ennifer Martin has been eating my brain since the second grade. Let me take you back in time a little.

Second grade. Summer and I were good friends with each other and everybody else, and not just from school, because we all went to the same toddler parks and kiddie gyms and library story hours together since forever. Back then everyone raved about Summer and me on account of I was dark haired and had dark eyes and Summer was very blond and had light blue eyes. Did I say this already? Well, the point is, we were so cute, and it's not just me saying that.

In walked Jennifer Martin, the "new girl." Jennifer also had blond hair, but hers was curly. Not as curly as mine, which can look like an explosion in a mattress factory in bad humidity (and this is Indiana, don't forget), but more curly than

Summer's, which was straight, except for the perm, which hadn't happened yet. Actually, the day Jennifer arrived, Summer's hair was green because of an unfortunate chlorine miscalculation at the YWCA swimming pool.

Jennifer had great clothes that her mom matched with socks, barrettes, shoes, and anything else that could accessorize the basic second grader on the go. And not the usual discount store jumpers and jeans you get because you outgrow stuff so fast. We found out (because Jennifer told us) that her mom went to Chicago for Jennifer's stuff. Like, Marshall Field's. You know?

I remember so perfectly that first day. Mrs. Knudsen was making this big thing about Jennifer and how she'd just moved into Glenwood and how we should all make her feel welcome and everything. She did that for all new kids, but the big deal she made over Jennifer was just a *lit*-tle bigger than her general tendency to make big deals out of everything.

You tell me, okay? The information about Jennifer's older brother being on *The New Mickey Mouse Club* and how Jennifer was taking voice and modeling and had been in the Chicago Civic Light Opera's·production of *The Nutcracker*? It seemed like kind of more than second graders needed to know at the moment. To me, anyway.

Mrs. Knudsen made sure Jennifer had a seat up front on the "story rug" and that Jennifer was right in the middle of the lunch table, where she could be totally seen from either end. Jennifer's advantageous geopositioning didn't make all that much difference to Summer and me. Although I freely admit, the matching accessories were troubling to me right from the start.

Other eyes were also on Jennifer that first day. Four of them, which belonged to Heather and Blair, a set of girl twins in our class.

Don't you think that's kind of weird, in a genetic way? Not that they're twins, but that there are two sets of twins in the same class? I mean, considering the limited population base in Glenwood and the statistical unlikelihood of it. You're always hearing about weird things happening in small towns because the water is polluted, or something like that.

Anyways, unlike Rod & Tod, Heather and Blair took baths on a regular basis and generally demonstrated good grooming all through grade school, which proved to me that the thing with Rod & Tod had nothing to do with being twins.

Now, it could be said that Summer and I did call Heather and Blair "Bleather and Hair" a few times more than we should have in the second grade. It started as an unfortunate slip by Mrs. Knudsen during attendance. It was funny, but it's nonetheless true that one can carry these things too far, and maybe we did. So all I'm saying is, I can't entirely blame them for turning to the dark side.

About two weeks after Jennifer started school was the first time we discovered that there was all of a sudden not enough room for us on the jungle gym. Jennifer, Blair, and Heather needed to have the whole jungle gym to themselves so they could sit up on the top and whisper about people. We were told that it was all about "safety rules" and everything. Like, I guess you're not supposed to have too many people sitting on the jungle gym and whispering at one time. Anyway, Miss Terry would point us toward some other activity.

Miss Terry. Right.

Miss Terry was actually this girl from high school who was getting extra credit as a classroom aide two days a week. Everybody thought she was cool because of being in high school. The next thing we knew, she was working for Jennifer.

She got hired to stay with Jennifer on weekends when Jennifer's mother would fly to Orlando to be with Jennifer's *New Mickey Mouse Club* brother. So Jennifer had Miss Terry all to herself, like her personal slave. The last time I saw Miss Terry was at Jennifer's birthday party when she was eight (Jennifer, I mean. Miss Terry was seventeen).

Jennifer had the usual stuff she had every year at her parties, the bouncing castle in her backyard, a magician, and Betty the Balloon Lady. Plus paper plates that matched the cake *and* matched Jennifer's party dress, too, and I don't mean just kind of matched.

Guys from *The New Mickey Mouse Club* were supposed to be there, too, but didn't make it because of bad weather in Orlando. And Miss Terry was there.

Jennifer's mom hired her to help out. Except by then, Miss Terry had gone all glassy-eyed and pale without a will of her own anymore. Kind of like a zombie with an ice-cream scoop. *"Must serve Jennifer. Must serve Jennifer."*

Jennifer always invited everybody to her birthdays, because it gave her a chance to let you know how important or unimportant you were. You knew this by how close you sat to her when it came time to cut the cake. Heather and Blair were the closest, usually sitting on either side of her. Most of the time Summer and I were at the far end of the table. Once she was going to make James Cunningham sit in the garage, but her mother wouldn't let her.

So, we are taking our seats at the complete other side of the long table when Jennifer goes, "I want Summer up here with us."

And, of course, zombied-out Miss Terry immediately came up with an extra chair to the right of Jennifer (shifting Heather over to Blair's side).

Summer looked at me and started to say, "No way, I'm sitting with Marci."

Or, at least I'm sure that's what she was *going* to say, but she didn't get the chance. Jennifer's mom just led her away and plopped her down next to Jennifer.

Summer did appear to have a good time next to the birthday girl, but I don't hold that against her. Summer always tries to make the best out of any given situation. Her persevering skills are much better than my own—something that will become obvious before this chapter is over.

The interesting thing about Miss Terry is that right after the above-mentioned birthday party, Jennifer got a new babysitter, who was the high school homecoming queen that year. Miss Terry, on the other hand, got mono, then moved away, and nobody ever saw her again. How spooky is that?

After the birthday party thing, Summer started to chub out and became not a good fashion match for Jennifer, who was never going to chub out or experience the accordion effect or anything else, and didn't care to have people around her who did have those problems.

Jennifer went from being this cute, slender fifth grader to

being this cute, slender sixth grader with a bra, excuse me. Now she's this cute, slender ninth grader who, even though she's fourteen like the rest of us, looks sixteen and hangs out with juniors just because she can and goes out on dates with guys who have their own cars!

It's just that girls like Jennifer get everything in life without ever having to take a number and wait. Then there're girls like Summer and me, which brings me back to where we were on the morning of March 22.

"Tell me if this hurts, Marci," Dr. Payne said to me with those weird bug-eyed glasses on and one of those masks that make you feel like you've got such utterly bad breath that he had to wear a mask to protect himself.

"Arrrgah!!! Urts!!! Ahhhh! Urts, urts!!!"

"You've been drinking sodas, haven't you, Marci?" he said as if the subject had moved on from when he was asking about what might hurt me. "Remember, we discussed sodas and what they do? Do you want your bands to oxidize?"

I hated when he asked me questions and carried on whole big conversations as he put his entire hand in my mouth, plus several of those sucker things and some tools that look like you could build bridges with them.

"Ahh . . . urgh . . . ahhh . . . ha," said I, holding up my end of the conversation.

"That's right," he answered, "because the oxidation will eat into the tooth enamel, leaving you with ugly discolored teeth that will destroy any hope you might have for a normal life."

The picture just over his shoulder of ugly discolored teeth

with holes in them lent silent support to this or anything else Dr. Payne might say in regard to my mouth.

All of this stuff going on was very mentally fatiguing, partly because the whole time I was also worrying about the Spring Fling dance and the looming and very real possibility of another year of humiliation against the wall. Also, there was the thing about the fake spit, as if Summer needed any additional stress in life at this particular moment. I was hoping nothing else would happen.

"Chew these, please," said Dr. Payne as he removed his fist from my mouth.

Uh-oh. Disclosion tablets.

"I promise to brush better."

"And these will help you," he said, "by turning your teeth black everywhere you've missed. You want to know where your plaque traps are, don't you, Marci?"

"Seriously, I know where my plaque traps are and I brush everywhere they are." He looked unconvinced. I added, "Lots," to prove my total commitment to this.

"Well," said Dr. Payne as he stood before a picture of ugly teeth, "if you brush, massage your gums, and floss adequately, you have nothing to worry about, do you?"

I glanced at the ugly teeth pictures.

"But if you're less than truthful, disclosion tablets will tell the story."

I reached for the tablets and slipped them into my mouth. You're supposed to chew, suck, and swish them around. Then, in a wonder of modern science right up there with fake spit, they turn your teeth black everywhere you missed with your toothbrush. *Except*, no matter how much you brush, and I always brush a lot before an appointment, they will always turn your teeth black. It's obviously this whole big dentist manipulation thing.

It is very hard to argue that you are capable of managing your own oral hygiene issues when you have totally black teeth. Therefore, robbed of your credibility, you surrender all authority to your dental care provider. To make sure you do not forget who is in charge of your mouth, you are not given enough time to rinse, so your teeth remain black for all the world to see.

Luckily, the ladies' room is right down the hall from the orthodontist (who is in the Glenwood Medical Arts Building). Unluckily, so are a lot of other doctors, including the one that does all the school athletic stuff.

I left the office acting like nothing was wrong and that I had my hand covering my mouth for no particular reason. Once out the door, I bolted for the ladies' room.

Wouldn't you just know it, half the guys from the JV track team were coming in for hydro muscle therapy or whatever they come there for and were heading right at me.

With my mouth ready for Halloween, I had no choice, so I turned and slammed my face against the wall to wait for them to go by. In the process, I hit my nose so hard, I thought it was going to bleed. I used my other hand to cover my nose, just in case.

A freshman girl without a figure and smashed up against the wall wasn't worth looking at, thank God. They didn't stop or ask if I hurt my nose or anything. Sometimes I'm grateful not to be noticed.

Running out of hands to cover stuff with, I got into the ladies' room and hung my head under the faucet. After rinsing and swishing about twenty times and scrubbing a little with my pointer finger, I could finally look at myself in the mirror and smile. And except for the braces, I looked okay. My nose was okay, too. As okay as it ever is.

I'd managed to get through forty-five minutes of being in public without anything getting done to me that was all that embarrassing. Not a bad day, so far. I turned around to go get Summer. She got me instead.

Ka-blam! There used to be a sign that said OPEN DOOR SLOWLY. I don't know what happened to it.

"Oh, Marci! God, I'm so sorry!" she said, or something like that. I couldn't understand her too well on account of she had her hand over her mouth and I was seeing stars.

"I just ran into half the JV track team out there!"

The second half. I ran into the first half.

Summer was genuinely concerned about smashing me, because she is a caring person. However, her teeth were black and sometimes you have to make choices. She hung her head under the faucet and started to swish. For all she knew, the third half of the JV track team could be waiting outside.

When my eyes refocused, I saw blood running down my lip. My nose had not escaped a second time.

At the start of Spring Fling there's a parade around the old-town square, by the lawn mower repair shops and past Hidden Treasures. It's one of the few times that people hang out there. Usually everyone's at the mall.

When Summer and I were little, our families used to come to the Spring Fling parade and we would sit together and everything. Once we were in it as part of Miss Vicky's Dance Class and wore hula skirts. The parade seemed real big to us back then, maybe because it was bigger, or maybe because we were littler.

Now it's kind of, like, if you've seen one clown on a unicycle, you've seen them all. Still, we can't resist going by to check it out. It's a tradition.

"I'm sorry about the door and everything, Marci," Summer said as we walked along the old-town square. She was adjusting her twin ponytails, which was her signature post-winter look.

"Dat's okay, Sumber."

My nose wasn't broken, but it wouldn't stop bleeding. This forced me to walk with my head back while pinching my nose with wet paper towels. I couldn't see much of the parade that was going on, but I did get a good look at the banner that hung across the street. That's why I remember the date so well—March 22.

"I was almost killed this morning," said Summer as she steered me around a Kiwanis-sponsored trash receptacle.

Even though *I* was the one with the nosebleed and also the one who might have a concussion, I was interested. The fact that Summer spoke calmly about almost being killed would never make me think that she wasn't truly almost killed. Like I said, she has good persevering skills.

"When?" I asked while dabbing my nose and making a mental note not to fall asleep for at least six hours.

"At the orthodontist's. Julie almost X-rayed my brain."

Surprising, because I knew Julie to be a nice person and a well-trained oral hygienist.

"She was doing an X ray on my upper left because I might have a cavity behind a spacer. You know?"

I did know.

"And she gets this phone call from her caterer, because she's getting married. You know?"

I knew that, too.

"And she leaves the X-ray thingie pointed right at my brain."

"At your actual brain?"

"Uh-huh," said Summer who had aligned her twin ponytails with geometric precision while walking and without the aid of a mirror, which nobody else I know of can do. She probably got that ability from her dad. He's unusually precise.

"It was pointed like that." She pointed her finger at her head like it was a gun or something.

I had to admit that even though she was a well-trained and nice person, Julie had been distracted by her approaching wedding, so it was a total possibility.

"How come you didn't go, 'Julie, you're gonna X-ray my brain,' or something? I would have."

"I had my finger in my mouth, holding the X-ray film in place, and they're always like, 'Don't move or anything.'"

"Yeah, but Summer, it was your brain, for crying out loud."

"Well, yeah," she admitted. "But Julie noticed before I got irradiated. She said it was her fault, what was I gonna say? She's a nice person, basically."

Summer was always willing to give people a break.

"Summer?" I asked, because things like getting your brain X-rayed had been on my mind. "Does it seem to you that weird stuff is always happening to us?"

"Like what?"

"Like today I almost got my nose broken, you almost got your brain irradiated, and we both got our teeth turned black. And it's not even ten o'clock yet. Doesn't that seem weird to you?"

"Compared to what?"

She had a point.

"Girlfriends! Hi!" The bubbly gush of a greeting came from a pink marshmallow perched on the back of a new Mustang convertible from Buckminster Ford of Glenwood with Mr. Buckminster himself driving. The pink marshmallow was Jennifer, as if you didn't know.

Mr. Buckminster eased the Mustang over to the curb right in front of us, somehow knowing what Jennifer desired him to do without her having to actually say it.

"I love it that we happened to meet up this way!"

Of course she did. She was on the back of a really cool car, wearing a poofy pink gown and a sash that said JR. MISS INDIANA and we were on the sidewalk, fighting off nose bleeds and sweating out concussions.

"As you know, the Spring Fling carnival starts tonight with the big dance. Exciting rides, valuable prizes, and celebrity guests!" She handed us a flyer.

"Like who?" inquired Summer before I could stop her.

"Like me."

The flyer confirmed this. "SPRING FLING" in big letters with her puffy pinkness pictured in the middle, smiling a smile that outshone the brand-new Mustang. And this, may I add, is without the benefit of any orthodontic adjustments whatsoever.

"I'm being honored for winning Junior Miss Indiana," she explained, answering a question that neither one of us had asked. "Some others are being honored, too. They're listed at the bottom."

And for sure, other names were supposed to be at the bottom. However, the bottom was chopped off and the only name remaining was "The Donut King." Actually it read THE DONUT KING, but we knew what it was supposed to be.

"They got chopped off due to an error in printing, I'm afraid," she said, double checking her picture on the flyer. "So I ended up on the flyer all by myself."

"Except for The Donut King," said Summer, who generally sees the positive side of things. "He didn't get chopped off. Not totally, anyway."

"Really?" She took the flyer back and examined it closely. "Hmmm," she said, making some kind of mental note to herself.

"Unfortunately, and here's the sad part," she said, just in case we didn't notice her concern, "my neighbor needs someone to baby-sit her Lhasa apso who just had this very serious dog surgery. Of course, I can't do it because I'm being honored and because I have a date, Randy Frasier. You probably don't know him because he's a junior. On the JV track team?" Then she looks at me and goes, "Oh, was that you smashed against the wall in the Glenwood Medical Arts Building this morning,

Marci? It sounded like you. They were all laughing because—"

"Jennifer," I interrupted. "I'm leaving in about ten seconds, even if you don't get to the point."

"Maybe you wouldn't mind passing up the dance to help out my neighbor's unfortunate Lhasa apso. You could order pizza and rent some videos and probably have just as good a time." She smiled and added, "Better, even."

If she hadn't said, "Better, even," this might not have happened. I was maintaining pretty well up to that point. But the suggestion that Summer and I would have a better time with a sick Lhasa apso than we would have at a dance made something in my brain snap.

"We'd love to help you out, Jennifer, but we have dates, too."

Okay. Some people might think that was a lie. I prefer to think of it as a *future truth*. I was sure that Summer and I would probably have dates at some point in our lives. So, it *was* true, just not at that particular moment.

It was pretty clear what Jennifer thought as her smile widened and her big blue eyes twinkled. I couldn't tell much about Summer because her face had locked up. You know, the way a computer screen does sometimes when you hit the wrong keys and it freezes.

"Really?" said Jennifer. "Who?"

"Hmm?" I asked, as if forgetting what I had just said.

"Who are your dates?"

"Oh. These . . . guys." Then I added, "That we know. And you don't," which I hoped would explain everything.

Summer fainted once in the sixth grade from low blood

sugar, so I stepped a bit closer to her in case I had to grab her. At the same time, I tried to match Jennifer's smile, but I'm not as good at it. My eyebrows usually always give away my innermost thoughts, which, at the moment, were, *What have you done, you moron!*

"That is so great, Marci," Jennifer said. "So I guess I'll see you tonight. You and Summer and your—dates." There was just enough of a pause before *dates* to indicate what totally big trouble we were in.

She gave us a little parade wave as the Mustang pulled away, making room for Brownie Troop 245, which had been patiently marching in place, waiting for Jennifer to move on.

Is it possible for somebody to die standing up? I wondered this, on account of Summer. She had this smile that was wide enough to catch the glint of her uppers, but her eyes were totally fixed and dilated.

"Well, I guess we shut her up, all right," I said. Then to counteract whatever my eyebrows were doing, I added, "Boy, that was great!"

"You know, Marci," Summer said as she slowly returned to this time-space continuum, "you are so right about how weird things are happening to us all the time. Like, it does seem kind of weird that you would tell Jennifer that we have dates. Especially when she so knows that we don't! *And she is so going to be telling everyone you said we did!!! And everybody is so going to be laughing at us tonight that* I'M NOT EVEN GOING TO GO!!!"

She stomped off, crossing the street and pushing her way right through Brownie Troop 245. Summer was usually respectful of Troop 245 because we were founding members. It was an indication of just how upset she was, and with very good reason.

I had set into motion the wheels of fate that could prove to be our most ultimate humiliation ever. Little did I know that other wheels of fate were being set into motion, too.

Summer stomped off down the street and right by Hidden Treasures, where a sign hung in the window. CLOSED.

Summer didn't notice and neither did I because we suddenly had humiliation issues. But if we had noticed, we would have wondered about it. Doris loves parades and festivals and hardly ever misses one.

The door was locked and the lights were off. The only sounds were from the constant ticking of all the old clocks she had (two mantels, six cuckoos, and one grandfather) and "This Land Is Your Land," which Brownie Troop 245 started singing as they passed the shop.

On the countertop was a newspaper, folded back to the classified ads. One had been circled.

```
$$$ ESTATE SALE $$$
Lots of Collectibles!!!
Many from Europe!!!
Everything must go!!!
```

Years of collecting junk was about to pay off for Weird Doris, in such a weird way that nobody could have imagined it.

3

Doris

$\mathcal{I}$ could have run after Summer, but I decided not to. It was better to let her take a Midol and lie down. She wouldn't stay at home for too long, anyway, on account of her bedroom was getting fogged for ants (the result of a slumber party the week before and some bean dip). And even if her room wasn't getting fogged, we both had to be at Doris' shop, Hidden Treasures, at noon. It's like, this job we got by accident in the seventh grade. And no matter how pissed off (with good reason) or potentially humiliated Summer might be at any given moment, she is always very dependable and rarely carries personal issues into the workplace.

The accidental job to which I refer happened during "Equal Opportunities for Women and Minorities in Business

Day" at James Monroe Middle School (aka Marilyn Monroe Middle School, unofficially). But it had more to do with me having a heat rash than with equal opportunities.

Only one of the six minority business guys could make it, Mel Ching, who owns The Donut King. The eighth grade had first choice and they took him because he brought doughnuts. There're five businesswomen in Glenwood, three in real estate and one in telemarketing. Other classes got them first. The fifth one was on vacation. Then somebody remembered Doris, who nobody had thought of (the story of her life), and our class got her.

So Doris gave this talk to the class about what it was like to be in her business. She brought different things from her shop as examples of what people tossed out but were actually of great value sometimes, if you thought about it. A pretty big *if*, in my opinion.

"Sometimes," she said, "you have to look really closely at something to see its value. And it turns out quite often that those are the things we cherish most. This is why I call my shop Hidden Treasures." And everybody is all, like, "Oh . . . is *that* why." As if they had ever wondered about it.

At the end she told us she had a real neat surprise. It was close to lunchtime and I, for one, was hoping the "neat" surprise was that we were getting out early. I was being driven nuts by this rash under my right arm. I had some stuff to stop the itching, but I had to reach under my shirt to smear it on and that meant getting to the girls' rest room.

I was unobtrusively lifting my arm to scratch at the same time Doris said, "I'd like to offer one or two of you children a chance to enter the world of business by working for me after school a couple of days a week."

I didn't really even know what she'd said, but I did notice that it was suddenly real quiet in the room. When I glanced up, I saw Summer looking at my right hand, which, being attached to my right arm, was up in the air while I was scratching. Next thing I knew, Mr. Hamlin was congratulating me on being so eager.

"That is so cool for you, Marci," said Jennifer, in that smiley sort of way she has that puts an unspoken *not* at the end of her occasional compliments. Then she explained to Doris that she herself had no extra time because of rehearsals for *Annie* and that she was Annie. Doris didn't know Jennifer and was thus confused.

Me? I was completely lost on account of how fast this all happened.

Now comes the very cool part, and to get why, you have to understand something. Summer didn't know that this had anything to do with heat rash. For all she knew, I had lost my mind and totally humiliated myself by volunteering to work in a junk store owned by somebody generally known as Weird Doris.

"Anybody else?" asked Mr. Hamlin.

Summer slowly raised her hand. She did it even though Blair and Heather had started whispering, smirking, and sharing looks about me with Jennifer. Summer wouldn't let me be humiliated all by myself.

This is why Summer and I are friends and always will be.

You might have noticed that I didn't call this chapter "Weird Doris." Just "Doris." Because once you get to know Doris, it's easy to see that the basis of her many interrelated problems, while weird on the surface, is understandable.

See, the thing about Doris is that when she was in the tenth grade she had to leave school to have a kidney transplant. And then, of course, she couldn't go back because of her fragile condition. That makes her bad hair, lack of fashion sense, and general dorkiness pretty understandable.

With an incomplete high school experience, you never get up on what's cool and what's not and the way to act at any given moment. You could just look at Doris and know she never got that kind of information.

I'm not saying you have to be a slave to fashion. Some people might even say that if Doris wants to be funky, that's totally fine. I personally don't know any people who would say that, but that doesn't mean they aren't out there . . . somewhere. What I *am* saying is, hers was not an informed choice.

It's like, have you seen a Picasso painting? My personal opinion doesn't matter here, because there are lots of people who like his stuff. However, you better believe that Picasso knew how to paint normal first and then *decided* to get strange. Both Doris and Picasso are weird; it's just that Doris never planned it that way.

For working at Hidden Treasures, we got paid the same as the current "baby-sitting rate" around Glenwood. Which, of course, meant we didn't have to baby-sit anymore, and that was fine with me, not being a baby person. Summer has historically been more maternal. However, on her second baby-sitting job, the tike she was watching secretly ate dog food just before his parents went to the movies (without turning their pager on, which makes me think they knew). There was no danger of poisoning because it was a premium brand, but if you've ever had partly digested dog food thrown up on you, and then also had to deal with the part that was fully digested, you can certainly understand Summer's preference for the junk business.

Our job was mostly sorting through stuff Doris bought at yard sales around central Indiana and separating the junk that's good from the junk that's junk. There's really a fine line and I gotta confess, I don't have it totally down, even now.

Okay, yes. Some things were easy to decide on. Like, she got these two rats whose names were Spike and Scooter. So, of course there wasn't a question about not tossing living creatures into the Dumpster, or things like Lava lamps that still worked, or cassettes by anybody you heard of, or anything autographed by someone that was dead.

When it came to things like a night-light that had a fake metal knight on it (get it? "knight light"), well, it was kind of up to Doris. The light didn't work and the joke wasn't that great. She kept it anyway. Go figure.

I should give Spike and Scooter their own chapter because of how important they get to be. But they weren't all that important as rats, and that's all they were for a really long time.

Doris got them at a yard sale across the street from James Cunningham's. They happened to be there, probably because James's mother had warned him to take better care of them or she was going to give them away. He didn't and they got walked across the street.

The lack of care most likely had something to do with cleaning the cage. James has deviated septums, which impairs his sense of smell. They probably got enough to eat, because they were alive and everything, although maybe they had to eat whatever they could get.

Three times that we can remember, James had come to school and been, like, "My rats ate my homework." A lame excuse? Hard to say because rats will eat anything. Summer had one in her garage once (wild, not tame) and it ate the fan belts right off her mom's Voyager.

Like I said, though, Spike and Scooter in rat form were only slightly interesting to Summer (who generally likes small creatures) and less to me. Although I was glad that the little guys now had a chance at a better life.

I sat at a table outside The Donut King, with a chocolate chocolate chip muffin and a Sprite. So deep was my despair that I would have gone for Triple Brownie Fudge Overload (which usually fixes me up pretty good), except 31 Flavors didn't open until noon. And besides that, The Donut King was on the route that we generally take on our way to Doris' shop. I was hoping to intercept Summer.

"Yoo-hoo! Marci!"

Also the route most likely to be taken by Doris, who was returning to her shop. She eased her 1972 Cadillac El Dorado convertible over to the curb beside me. It's the second-oldest car in Glenwood and the absolute longest. She got it at a yard sale. Though an environmental abomination, the "cushion air ride" is easy on her transplanted kidney.

"Want a ride?"

"Waiting for Summer," I answered.

"Know where I've been?"

"To a yard sale?"

"Estate sale. But I forgot to take the paper that had the address," she said with her little laugh.

Doris worries about short-term memory loss.

"You know, Marci, short-term memory loss is the thing that worries me the most as I get older."

Maybe she never heard about varicose veins.

"Took me all morning to find it. How was the parade?"

"Awesome," I answered, not wanting to disappoint her. I took another bite of chocolate chocolate chip muffin and waited for the endorphins to kick in.

"We have a lot of work to do today," she said with a kind of glee that lit up her eyes and caused her Coke bottle glasses to glow.

I looked at the trunk of her car. If it was full, it was going to be an all-afternoon thing. You can play racquetball in the trunk of a 1972 El Dorado.

Her hair was particularly bad, and I hoped she had worn a hat while she was out in public. Or maybe she had been wearing a hat and had just taken it off. If she had worn the hat for nine hours, that would account for the hair.

"Were you wearing a hat?"

"No. Why?" There are four mirrors in her El Dorado. You'd think she would look in at least one of them.

"No reason," I said with a sigh. I just didn't feel like going into it yet again. It's not like Summer and I hadn't tried and tried.

"Know what else I got?"

"ABBA eight tracks?" "Dancing Queen" was currently playing on the El Dorado's built-in eight track, and Doris was a known sucker for Disco, it being the last popular music she remembers before she left high school and her social evolution came to a dead end.

"No, *this*!"

She held out this little gold box. It was obviously fake gold, and Doris knew that from her knowledge of secondhand stuff. There was something else about it she liked.

"Listen." She leaned way out of the driver's side window and shook the little box. It rattled. Anything that rattled was like catnip to Doris.

"There's something inside."

"What?"

"I don't know."

"Why don't you open it and see?"

"It's locked."

"Why don't you unlock it?"

"There's no key."

You know, when you have a lot on your mind, like just having made a fool out of yourself and your best friend, this kind of conversation can be really annoying.

"What did you pay for the box, Doris?"

"Seventy-five cents."

That was a relief. Although my two years in the junk

business told me it could have been had for a quarter.

"You seem a tad bellicose this morning, Marci," she said, emphasizing *bellicose.*

Two months before she had bought some books by the pound. One was *Word Wealth: Sixty Days to a Stronger Vocabulary.* The sixty days were just about up, and her vocabulary was definitely stronger. So was mine from just being around her.

"Jump in. We'll go to the shop and see what's inside the box."

"Doris, I don't have to be there until noon. Okay? And right now I got more important stuff to worry about than an old box."

She was right. I was bellicose.

She smiled, because she always does, no matter what. "Okay," she said, and pulled the El Dorado into drive. It made the usual *chunk* sound. She waved and pulled away.

Great. Perfect. I can't say anything to anybody anymore, I thought. Everyone hates me.

The chocolate chocolate chip muffin was almost gone and I felt even worse.

Then the Donut King's wife, whose name is Lu Ching, stepped out to ask me if I wanted anything else. It was so kind of her. She was pregnant and looked very happy.

"Will this be your first child?" I asked, suddenly very sad that I wasn't a baby person, which only proved how utterly miserable I was as a person and how everyone should hate me.

"Yes," she said, "my husband has always wanted a son."

All I could think of was how much my bands were oxidizing from drinking a soda, and how much I cause my own and Summer's humiliation all the time, and how much I'm not a baby person. My life sucked.

"Something wrong?" asked Lu Ching, who was probably never bellicose to anyone.

"No, not really," I said, dabbing tears with my napkin, "but do you think 31 Flavors might open early, on account of the parade?"

"I can check for you."

"Thank you so much," I squeaked.

Then I blew my nose, which is the ceremonial end to most crying jags. This one wasn't too bad.

"Marci?" It was Summer. She noticed my red eyes and instantly apologized for yelling.

It was, like, *she,* who had done nothing except become understandably hysterical, was apologizing to *me*, the person who was totally to blame. I started tearing up all over again.

"No, Summer. You were so right. I did a terrible thing and caused pain to you, my best friend." Summer started to tear up, too.

"31 Flavors is open now," said Lu Ching, sticking her head out the door.

"Really?" asked Summer, surprised because it wasn't noon yet.

"I just want you to know, Summer, that I thought it all over, and I have an idea about how we can fix this so everything works out okay." I dabbed my eyes and added, "Or at least becomes somewhat acceptable."

Rod & Tod

"**I** can't believe that you're even suggesting this!"

"Summer, I said our dates were guys and these are guys." I tried to sound positive, which was difficult. Rod & Tod were wrestling on their front lawn and shouting things that sounded suspiciously like lines from *Hercules*.

"You said we had 'dates,' who were 'these guys,' that 'we knew and she didn't!' She so knows these guys! Okay?!"

"So, two out of three. What do you think, that Jennifer keeps score?" That was a stupid thing to say. Of course, Jennifer keeps score.

As the wrestling continued across the street, I tried another approach with Summer.

"And besides that," I started, as if I had already made one good point, "you said yourself that Tod calls you up sometimes."

"Yeah, to burp the alphabet! Like I wanna be seen with a guy who might start burping the alphabet at any second!"

It was true. Tod's claim to fame was burping the alphabet down to *Q* in one breath. Rod could only get to *H*. When they were little, Rod took piano. Tod took trumpet. That probably explains the difference, seeing as how, genetically speaking, they are carbon copies.

In the old days they were kind of cute. I'm talking second grade here. They even both got valentines from Jennifer and Blair and Heather. And it didn't really matter that they ate the candy hearts and the valentines fell on the floor, along with Summer's and mine.

Then, between fifth and sixth grade, nature played a very cruel trick on Rod & Tod. Just about the time the rest of us became aware of good grooming, Rod & Tod stopped taking showers. How socially uncoordinated is that?

They even bragged about running the water and getting the towels wet to fool their mom (who is probably highly mortified to read this). Where's the logic? They gotta spend ten minutes in the bathroom making noises; why not just take a shower? James Cunningham thought it was pretty cool, he of the deviated septums and extreme sinus blockage.

And Hot Dog Day? Charming. Starting in fifth grade, Rod & Tod, James Cunningham, and all of the rest of those guys turned Hot Dog Day in the cafeteria into this X-rated freak-out of lame jokes and gross remarks related to their hot dogs. Again, it's right at the time when Summer and I were, like, "Puh-leeze, we don't wanna hear about it."

* * *

"Hey!!!"

Summer flinched.

Hey! was their standard greeting. It was almost like they stabbed you with it. It was Tod who first spotted us.

"What are you guys doing here?"

I held on to Summer's sleeve. Half for support and half because I thought she might bolt.

"We want to ask you guys something."

Summer had turned beet red as her persevering skills utterly and totally failed her. Blondes like Summer change colors pretty easily like, to red and green. I'm sort of olive complected and so don't have to worry about blushing as much as Summer. Still, God only knows what my eyebrows were doing.

Tod had leaves sticking in his hair, and his shirt was soaked with sweat and dirt and looked like it had, at some point, been ironed with a brick. I was hoping they would come over together because I didn't want to go through this twice, but what can you do?

Tod was grinning, which I took to be a good sign, but before I could open my mouth to say anything, he goes, "You guys wanna see something really cool?"

"If it has to do with hot dogs, I'm leaving," Summer said in my ear. Sadly, it was a possibility.

"Okay, Tod, but I want to ask you something really serious," I said, "so can you, like, focus?"

"Sure, but watch this! It's totally cool!" And then he whistled really loud to Rod and I felt like I was going to suffer some hearing loss.

"Watch this!!!" yelled Rod as he spun his bike around.

I'm not kidding. As all of us watched, Rod zipped by us, screaming fake Japanese war cries, and slammed, full speed, into their neighbor's trash cans.

Tod started laughing hysterically and jumping up and down, shouting, "Too cool!"

"He crashed into the trash cans," I said, just to confirm that it was as intentional as it looked.

"Well, yeah. That's the really cool part!"

I wouldn't use the word *cool.* Although I will admit that it was kind of hard to take my eyes off it. Like a car wreck, when you don't want to look, but you can't help it.

Rod got himself up from the ground and started removing banana peels and empty yogurt containers and other stuff that had landed on him after he'd crashed into the trash can, and you just knew that later on, not only was he going to fake taking a shower, but he'd also probably try to get away with wearing the same clothes tomorrow.

"So, what did you want to ask us?" said Tod as Summer backed away.

"Never mind." I patted Tod on the arm and made a mental note to wash my hands before eating anything.

Bong.

The grandfather clock had just bonged the last of twelve bongs and, since it runs the slowest of all the clocks in Hidden Treasures, it meant that the Rod & Tod debacle had made us late for work. Doris didn't notice.

While we were watching Rod crash into trash cans, Doris

was in her shop, gathering up her collection of keys. She has keys for everything from roller skates to suitcases, so it was no big surprise that one of them opened the fake gold box.

Inside was a small ring, engraved with some kind of foreign writing. Doris was pretty used to fake jewelry because her shop is full of it, so it's not like she was really excited to find a crummy little ring.

However, the ad for the estate sale had said that some of the stuff was from Europe. Of course, they always say junk like that, and being a veteran of countless yard, garage, and rummage sales, Doris wasn't gullible in that respect. But still, there was that writing that went all the way around the ring.

Doris held the ring up to the light and squinted at the writing through her thick glasses, trying to make out the strange symbols. Being late, Summer and I weren't there while she was doing this. And I'm still a little confused about what happened next.

The only eyewitnesses were Spike and Scooter, who had spent the last six months on the shelf next to a 1947 gum-ball machine. Usually, if you want a pet, you don't go to the secondhand store, which explains why they were still there. But Spike and Scooter couldn't tell anyone what they saw in Hidden Treasures that morning because, being rats, they couldn't talk.

At least, they couldn't at that point.

Mood Swings

Summer was not only facing public humiliation because of me but was also grossed out by the admittedly poor Rod & Tod suggestion. She was also probably depressed because, grossed out or not, Rod & Tod had been our only date options. I know it depressed me. Lots.

"We could go by 31 Flavors," I offered.

"I don't wanna go by 31 Flavors!" And before I could suggest it, she added, "I don't wanna to take a Midol, either! I wanna put a bag over my head until I can find somewhere else to live!"

Because Summer is much taller than me, with much longer legs, a fast walk for her is like this trot for me. Out of breath, I stopped her just before she opened the door to Hidden Treasures. I just felt we had to bring some closure to this before going inside.

"I say we go to the dance. So we get laughed at a little, Summer. There are worse things."

"Like *what*, Marci?" she snapped.

Then my eyebrows shot right up to the top of my head. "Like that."

I pointed at Doris, who had just opened the door behind Summer. Summer turned back to see Doris and was suddenly, like, "Eeeek!"

Doris grinned at us from underneath a very tall pile of curls that cascaded down, falling all around her shoulders like some nightmare shampoo commercial.

She smiled and brought her finger to her lips. "Shhh."

She hustled us inside, looked up and down the street, turned her OPEN sign to CLOSED, and shut the door.

It wasn't so much that Doris had this Marge Simpson hair all of a sudden; it's the way she said she got the hair (not the way she said it, the way she got it).

"I wished for it and I got it," she said.

I was standing a little closer to Doris than Summer, and I could see that it wasn't a wig or some kind of clown hair that maybe fell off a clown during the parade. This was real, actual hair.

"Isn't it the strangest thing?"

I nodded and stepped back with Summer.

"Want to touch it?"

"No, that's okay, thanks anyway." We both took another step back.

"Notice anything else—different about me?"

Remember what I said about not being able to take your eyes off a car wreck? "Sorry, Doris, it's kind of hard to get past the hair."

"I don't need my glasses anymore!"

True enough, she wasn't wearing her glasses. She bolted across the shop to the counter at the far side where old radios and cameras got put. She grabbed this camcorder, turned it over, and looked at the bottom. "No user-serviceable parts inside. Opening case voids warranty!" Then she grinned and was all, like, "What do you think?"

We looked at each other. Then Summer goes, "Doris, it's pretty old and the warranty's probably no good, anyway."

"I'm not talking about the warranty!"

"Doris, you were talking about warranty," I said, not making any sudden movements. "Like, just a second ago."

"Forget about the warranty!"

"*You* brought it up," said Summer, transferring her annoyance with me to Doris.

"I was *reading* the warranty *because I can*! I can read anything!"

"You're free to read anything you want, Doris," I said. "It's not like this isn't America, you know."

"Without my glasses."

Summer and I were, like, "Oh."

Doris lifted the camcorder and looked at the little on-off switch that has *on* and *off* written on it, and she goes, "See? On, off, on, off, on." Then she started coming at us with it up to her eye, going, "Smile, Marci! Summer, yoo-hoo! I see you!"

She said that she had perfect vision because she wished for it. "And I think it's got something to do with this rrreeee-ing!" She meant *ring*, except she was singing it. Like, reee-ing. I think it's really annoying when people do that.

She put the camcorder down and held up her hand, and there was this little ring on her finger. To us it didn't look any different than other junky stuff she has around the shop.

She was talking really fast about strange writing that was probably from Europe because the newspaper ad said some of the stuff came from there. She pointed at the folded newspaper on the counter.

Europe usually gets blamed for a lot of weird stuff because they've got guys like Dracula in their cultural tradition. Still, a magic ring? Summer and I were understandably dubious.

"How else do you explain what's happened to me?"

Too many years of antirejection medication, I thought. Then out loud I said, "Maybe you just got your hair done like that, then forgot you did it."

"Totally understandable," Summer assured her in a soothing voice.

Doris explained that she had gotten the box open and found the ring inside. Then she had been rubbing it and stuff, polishing it, trying to see exactly what kind of ring it was. And she couldn't find the magnifying glass that she uses.

So far this made sense to us. She misplaces things a lot. And the first thing she ever does with any polishable item is polish it. So we're going, "Uh-huh."

"Then I put the ring on my finger and I hold it up to the light to try to get a better look."

And we're, like, "Makes sense."

"I said, 'I wish my eyes were perfect,' the way people do sometimes."

I don't, but on the other hand, I do talk to myself in the shower sometimes. So, it was still pretty believable.

"And then, right after I said, 'I wish my eyes were perfect,' my eyes were perfect."

That's when things got difficult for us as far as believability.

Doris goes, "I started looking all around the shop, testing my eyes." She got sort of creepy sounding and started moving around the shop, looking at everything and acting all dramatic.

"Then I saw myself in the mirror. My hair looked kind of funny, like I had been wearing a hat for about nine hours."

I nodded to Summer, confirming that Doris had had serious hat hair about thirty minutes before.

"I got distracted, trying to pat it down. So I said something like, 'I wish I had different hair. And . . . *poof.*'"

Looking at her hair, it did seem reasonable to believe that some kind of *poof* had been involved. But at that point, we thought it was more tragic than magic.

"Here, you try," she said, attempting to pull the ring off her finger.

"That's okay, Doris. We really don't need to."

The ring was stuck on her finger. She zipped into the bathroom, which was just behind the curtain that separated the shop from the back room part. We heard water running.

"If this happens to me in later life," whispered Summer, "shoot me."

Doris came back, rubbing her hand with soap. The ring slid off. She grabbed Summer's hand and put the ring in her palm and folded her fingers over it. "Wish, Summer! Anything you want!" She was so excited.

Summer looked at Doris. I looked at Summer. Spike and Scooter looked at all of us.

"Wish!" Doris whispered. *"Anything you want!"*

Summer isn't impulsive and tends to give even stupid stuff serious thought.

"Ooo-*kay*. I wish for . . ."

Her eyes looked around the shop as she thought. Everything was silent, except for the ticking of all the clocks and the little squeaky sounds from Spike and Scooter.

Summer took a breath. "I wish for a couple of cool guys to take us to the dance tonight *so we don't get laughed at.*" And she gave me this look!

"What's *that* supposed to mean?" I demanded.

"What?"

"Oh, right! That look you were so giving me just now!"

Because Summer kept acting like she didn't know what look I was talking about, this led to an argument, and neither one of us noticed Doris.

She was searching all around the shop for the two cool guys Summer wished for right before she gave me that look. But there weren't any cool guys, not in the back room, not in the storage closets, not in the bathroom, not anywhere.

"Give me the ring—maybe I have to do it!" And Doris grabbed the ring from Summer and started wishing for two cool guys for us. She kept wishing and looking and wishing and looking while we were arguing.

"The thing that so disappoints me, Summer," I said, "is that it was more important for you to wish some wish just so you could give me a look instead of wishing for world peace or something for orphans, which is what I, or any caring person, would have done!"

"There aren't any orphans around here!" she said, as if that was the point. Then we noticed Doris.

She was standing in the back room. Just standing there. Her arms were hanging down to her sides and she looked all, like, limp. Then she looked back at us, but the smile was gone. Summer and I knew all about mood swings and this one was major.

"I don't know why it's not working," she said in this totally confused way. "I got perfect vision and this hair the second I asked for it."

We wanted to say something like, "Let's try again later," or, "Maybe it needs batteries," or something. But that would be kind of like saying we believed the ring was magic when we so obviously didn't. And we didn't want to be condescending. We also couldn't say, "Don't be stupid, Doris, grow up," which would have been supercilious.

So we did probably the worst thing we could do. We just sort of stood there and looked at her.

Doris has this old recliner in the back room. It used to vibrate but doesn't anymore. She sank into it. Not like she was mad or anything. More like somebody let the air out of her.

"That's okay, Doris." I said.

"Yeah, it doesn't matter," Summer said.

Doris just looked at us with this expression that was so heartbreaking. We knew that expression all too well on account of we had seen it on each other's faces lots of times. Doris was humiliated.

What we should have said was, "Don't worry, Doris, we

get humiliated all the time." But to be really honest about it, bumping into doors, or having a mouth full of black teeth, or saying we have dates when we don't is a way different humiliation from going psycho.

So what's the most embarrassing thing that could happen right here? I mean, right at the very second when Summer and I couldn't say what we were really thinking, but Doris obviously knew what we were thinking, anyway.

"Cuckoo." It was twelve-thirty and the clocks were going off all around us. "Cuckoo, cuckoo, cuckoo." How embarrassing was that?

Summer was the first one to spring into action. "*Carlton Plaza* is on, Doris," she said. Summer can keep the *TV Guide* program grid for the entire week in her head and always knows what's on at any given moment (kind of like this science thing she inherited from her dad).

Summer leaped to the six old TVs that sit across from the recliner that doesn't vibrate. At least two will always get an okay picture; you just have to figure out which two because it's always different depending on the weather. Herb the Handyman wired them all up to this antenna on the roof.

Doris doesn't have, like, even basic cable. She disconnected it after the third rate hike in one year. She complained about it and wrote letters to the mayor and the city council. She never got an answer to any of them, not even the usual "Thank you for your concern" that they send to everybody, no matter what they complain about.

Herb the Handyman offered to put up an antenna for her, but he might have been distracted from being around her and not done such a good job. He had this thing for Doris, or so she thought. She was absolutely sure he was going to ask her out once. That was in 1973. Doris thought he might be working up to it.

While Summer turned on the various TVs, I was able to stop the last cuckoo clock from going off (it was always slow). Then I saw Spike and Scooter on the shelf. Doris thought they were cute and they made her laugh sometimes. So I pulled them down and took them into the back room.

"You can look at Spike and Scooter until Summer gets a TV to work, Doris." But Spike and Scooter just sat there. I banged on the cage, hoping they would do some funny stuff. They freaked out and hid behind their treadmill.

"You know, Doris," I said as Summer jiggled wires behind the TVs. "It's great that you can see without your glasses. Laser eye surgery is kind of expensive, and no matter how it happened, you saved a lot." Except it wasn't that great, maybe.

Without her glasses, I could see little lines around her eyes and stuff. She looked older without her glasses, and tired. She looked at me and smiled, so she wasn't in a coma or anything and that was good. But it wasn't a high-quality smile. You know?

"If you want to change your hairstyle, we can help you figure out some stuff to do with it." And I thought we actually could. Doris' hair had always been limp and lifeless. Now it was full of body, at least. Without too much trouble, it could go from a Marge Simpson to an okay sort of Anna Nicole Smith. "We can get some ideas from *Seventeen*, for sure,"

I said, just to let her know I was serious about it.

Carlton Plaza came on. The best picture was on a black-and-white TV, but the show was just starting, so that was good, and because it was Friday, it would be a climactic installment. They were showing what happened over the last week, which they do just before the first commercials.

"It's just starting, Doris," Summer said.

"That's great!" I said enthusiastically.

Then we both kind of stepped back by the recliner, like we were all interested and excited about it. Summer said, "Wow," which might have been a little too much.

There on the screen was Regina Leigh Savage, who played this woman named Monica who ran this big hotel. You never saw the hotel, like the lobby or the rooms, but judging by Monica's office, it had to be pretty awesome.

It was generally believed that Monica had poisoned her uncle, who used to own the hotel, which had been owned before that by Monica's father. Monica always thought it should have been hers and now it was, thanks to arsenic (the uncle was poisoned before we knew Doris and even heard of *Carlton Plaza*). Monica's cousin, George, showed up last November during Thanksgiving vacation and was all, like, "You poisoned my father and you'll regret it, you bitch!" They use realistic language, which is necessary for believability.

We helped Doris catch up with the story sometimes if she had missed a few episodes or just forgot due to short-term memory loss. We were usually in school when it was on but always watched when we were sick or on vacation.

So there was Regina Leigh Savage in her tailored Monica

outfit sitting at her desk (she's also very into Victoria's Secret stuff and has the figure for it). And there's George in her office, because it's the only place in the hotel they ever are, and he's going off on her about how he has this evidence. And Monica's looking down, glancing at something. Then they show what Monica is looking at and it's this gun in her desk drawer.

"Whoa!" said Summer. And I go, "It's a gun." And Summer goes, "Intense."

Even with that, Doris wasn't getting into it. We didn't know what else we could do.

"Would either one of you like something to eat?" Doris said it in this zombie way I hadn't heard since Miss Terry left town. "I haven't gone to the market this week, but I can make us Cup of Soup." She had a working microwave and we often had Cup of Soup together.

"No, that's okay. I had a chocolate chocolate chip muffin already." Then Summer and I did something that neither one of us are proud of in the least.

We said we knew that Doris really wanted to watch that installment of *Carlton Plaza* and everything, because it looked so climactic. And we said we had some other stuff to do, so we would come back later. Then Summer and I just kind of backed away and got out of there.

We left Doris alone with six cuckoo clocks, which would all go off again in a half hour, reminding her of what everybody in Glenwood thought about her and what we thought about her, too.

Incredible Simulations

*I*t's about a fifteen-minute walk from 31 Flavors to Summer's house. Summer and I don't ride bikes anymore because we don't like the way it makes our butts look. Actually Summer more than me, because she has a rounded figure, which looks pretty good everyplace *except* on a bicycle.

It was a long fifteen minutes because of how bad we both felt. It was hot for the middle of March and our single scoops of Triple Brownie Fudge Overload had melted into a kind of goop that we had to lick off the spoon in order to get the full chocolate benefit.

We tried to talk about the dance and how to extricate ourselves. *Extricate* is a very cool word meaning to disembarrass. It gives you so much hope in your darkest hours to know that there is a word like that, because why would there be unless disembarrassing yourself was something that was actually possible? But even as important as extrication was to us, we couldn't stop thinking about Doris.

Summer thought we should tell somebody about her. But tell them what? That she was weird? Everybody already knew that.

"Weirder," Summer said.

"Than what?"

Since seventh grade we had gotten to know her better than anybody except, maybe, Herb the Handyman. So we kind of knew the difference between *weird* and *weirder* as far as Doris was concerned. To everybody else, weird was weird and there was no more or less about it.

In times of boredom, or despair and uncertainty, we go to Summer's house and look through recent issues of *Seventeen* (Summer has more closet space, so we keep them there). It's not like it has the answers to everything, because it doesn't. Most answers in life come from within our own selves, with the exception of answers to specific style and grooming questions. It's just that Summer and I usually come up with the best answers from within when we aren't thinking too hard about whatever the humiliation of the moment is. That's where *Seventeen* comes in. It helps us not to think too hard about stuff by making us focus on skin care and how to have stronger nails in thirty days.

According to the directions on the ant fog can, it was safe to enter Summer's bedroom, but our feeling about these things is, why take a chance? So we held our breath, got the *Seventeen*s, and dragged lawn chairs out to the front yard. We couldn't go into the back because that's where Summer's mom, Judy, was feeding her plants. We didn't want her asking us if something was wrong. We hate that, especially when something *is* wrong.

We sat beside each other, flipping pages, which was the only sound there was for a long time. *Flip . . . flip . . . flip . . .*

I noticed that Summer's leg was bouncing up and down really fast. She had a lot to bounce her leg over, after all.

1. Jennifer had absolutely already spread the news about our nonexistent dates and everybody was going to be waiting to see them be nonexistent.
2. Not only were we going to be standing against a wall all night, but we were going to be laughed at while we did it.
3. Guilt over leaving Doris in a time of emotional crisis.
4. A large amount of chocolate in her system.

But there was something even more troubling on Summer's mind.

"Marci?"

"Yeah?" I was flipping even faster because I knew what she was going to say.

"Do you ever think that we might turn out to be like Doris?"

"That so won't happen, it's not worth talking about." I answered too fast, almost like screaming that inside I was thinking the very same thing. I just kept looking at our *Seventeens. Flip . . . flip . . . flip . . .*

"How do you know?" Summer asked.

"I just know."

"But how can anyone know? I bet even Doris didn't know she would turn out to be *Weird Doris.*"

"Summer!" Then, more calmly, I go, "We are way different from Doris."

"Different how?"

"In eight months for me and eleven months for you, we are going to have straight teeth and corrected jawlines. Doris, on the other hand, has a severe overbite. So, there's one big difference right there."

"Yeah, but name a more important difference."

"We've both got our own kidneys."

She started say something, and I said, "And don't go, 'We *might* lose a kidney,' because I would go, 'And MTV *might* come to Glenwood because it's sooo cool and put us on *The Real World,*' which is just about as likely as losing a kidney, in my opinion."

She thought about it, then said, "Why would MTV put us on *The Real World*?"

"Summer, that is not the point! Okay? So just be logical. We know how to dance and other stuff, too. And we get *Seventeen*, so we both have lots of preventive knowledge in regard to style mistakes. Doris never had that. I could go on and on about it, but those are the basic differences."

The truth was, I couldn't go on and on about it, which was scary to me. Usually I can go on and on about practically any-thing in life. But about us turning into a couple of Weird Dorises someday, the truth was I couldn't think of any real rea-son why that wasn't a total possibility. And the lie I told about us having dates was only going to speed the process along. I could feel these tears flooding up, and I wasn't the only one.

"I'll be back in a second," Summer said. I knew she was going to get the Kleenex box—for both of us.

But before Summer got two steps, something totally unexpected happened. And I mean, unexpected in the context of a whole morning's worth of unexpectedness.

"YOO-HOO!!!" Real loud like that.

Nobody says "yoo-hoo" in Summer's neighborhood, because the people are mostly college educated. So we turned to see who was yoo-hooing.

Doris' giant Cadillac came around the corner, bounced up on the curb, and whomped back down, giving the cushion air ride a workout.

"Yoo-hoo!!!"

The sun was bright, so it was hard seeing into the car. What we could make out was that Doris had changed her hairstyle again. At least it didn't look like a Marge Simpson, nor did it look like an Anna Nicole Smith. It was this total Regina Leigh Savage thing.

"Yoo-hoo!!! Girls!!!" she said as the El Dorado hit the curb, turning the wide white walls dingy gray in a split second.

"I'm getting my mom, Marci, on account of this is serious."

"Summer!" I said while I squinted into the car. She stopped and turned back to look.

"Oh . . . my . . . God . . ." kind of leaked from Summer.

Under the Regina Leigh Savage hair was Regina Leigh Savage herself, climbing out of the El Dorado. What's more, she was dressed in the tailored designer outfit she had been wearing on *Carlton Plaza* when last we saw her.

"Yoo-hoo!!!"

"She sounds like Doris," I said.

"But looks like Regina Leigh Savage," Summer said.

She walked toward us and tripped coming up the flag-stone path.

"But she walks like Doris," I said.

She threw her arms out wide sort of like a *"Ta-da"* thing. "What do you think?" she asked in Doris' voice.

What did we think? To have a popular daytime drama star right there on Apple Orchard Drive? And you know how people always say that guys on TV don't look that way in person? Well, Regina Leigh Savage did, exactly.

"Why are you in Doris' car?" asked Summer in a less than sanguinelike manner.

"Because *I'm* Doris."

"Doris is Doris," said Summer, who had a point.

"I can explain," said Regina Leigh Savage, sounding like Doris.

"You can try," I said, also not so sanguine anymore.

Regina Leigh Savage held up her hand, and there on her finger was the same ring Doris had at her shop.

"It *does* do something," she said, "but like so much in life, you have to know how it works."

"Wait a minute, Regina Leigh Savage," I said. "Summer wished for cool guys with that very same ring and we got zip. Okay?"

"Because," said she who claimed to be Doris, "you wished for cool boys out of the *thin air*. Do boys just pop up from nowhere?"

If you're Jennifer Martin, they do.

"It's not like an 'out of thin air' thing at all. It's like a *Cinderella thing*."

"Say what?"

"Did the Fairy Godmother get a coach and horses for Cinderella out of thin air? No. She had to *turn something into something*. So she turned some mice into horses and a pumpkin into a coach."

"And you turned yourself into popular daytime drama star Regina Leigh Savage, I suppose." I had gone from not being sanguine to being very incredulous.

"Well, not all at once. After you left, I asked myself, why did I receive good vision and amazing hair but didn't get the guys you wanted? At first I thought, maybe I only got three wishes. With the vision and hair, maybe two boys added up to four wishes. So I wished for one boy that you could share. But nothing happened."

That was kind of a relief.

"Then I thought," she said, acting like she was thinking really hard. "My eyes? My hair? Don't you get it?"

I can't say that we did.

"I already had eyes and hair! My accidental wishes just *transmuted* them," she said, emphasizing *transmuted* the way Doris did with *Word Wealth* words.

"So I stood up to try it again but fell over the rats." Then she looked at me and said, "Somebody left the cage right in the middle of the floor."

"I was trying to make you feel better—don't be grateful or anything." Then, clarifying, "Make *Doris* feel better, I mean."

"I twisted my ankle and it hurt really badly," she said,

pointing to her left foot, which was in a simple yet elegant pump with a three-inch heel. "This was right at the time when Monica shot George on *Carlton Plaza.*"

"I *knew* she was going to shoot him!" exclaimed Summer, who had gotten slightly off track.

"So Regina Leigh Savage, as Monica, is saying to George, 'A lot of people wish they had my nerve.' Nerve to shoot him, I suppose. And I'm rubbing my ankle and say, 'I wish I had your legs,' and poof, I had her legs, which came with panty hose and heels. Pretty strange, huh?"

"What about the whole rest of you, the body and face?"

"I'm telling you girls, and this is the truth," she said, leaning and kind of whispering. "Once you start transmutating things, it is very hard to stop."

"And the designer outfit?" asked Summer, now back on track.

"I don't know," answered the person claiming to be Doris. "Perhaps it's like Barbie."

That sort of made sense. Barbie always comes with at least one outfit.

"If you're Doris, prove it," said Summer.

"Well," she said thoughtfully, "who else besides Doris drives a 1972 semirestored El Dorado convertible?" And she walked back to the car and pointed at it like she had made this superbig point.

"You could have stolen it," Summer said, although logically nobody would.

"I know the meaning of *transmutated*," she said with pride.

"Lots of people have *Word Wealth: Sixty Days to a Stronger Vocabulary*," I said. Then Summer and I walked right down to her and folded our arms and I go, "Tell us something that only Doris would know."

"You two are desperate for dates because you don't have any and you said you did."

Summer freaked out. "Everyone totally knows, like everybody in town, and now everybody on television, too!!!"

"Wait, I'm not finished." And Regina/Doris walked back to the El Dorado.

"No, but *we're* finished, Marci! Swear to God, I am totally moving to another town!"

Meanwhile, Regina/Doris had reached in and pushed the button that lowers the convertible top on the massive car. *Bzzzzzz.*

And Summer was still all, like, "I don't know who she is, but I'm just a kid and shouldn't have to be dealing with this stuff." It was chocolate rebound talking.

"Mom!" she yelled. *"Mom!!!"*

"Oh, girls. Look what I have for you," cooed Regina/Doris.

"SUMMER!" I said, seeing what was in the backseat. Except I didn't yell it. I whisper-yelled it, like, *"Summmmmmer!!!"* But that made no difference to her.

"No!" she said. *"No 'Summer, stop it!' No 'Summer, take a Midol!' No, no, NO!"*

This is like, the place in the movies where they throw a glass of water in the person's face so they calm down. There was only a garden hose in the front yard, and thank God I didn't have to use it. Summer suddenly saw the same thing I did.

There are times in your life, I'm beginning to find out, when even *Word Wealth* fails you. This was one of them. Because when that car top was finally down enough that we could see into the backseat . . . Well, what can I say? There sat two of the cutest guys I have ever seen in my whole life— and that includes major motion pictures. Obviously Summer thought the same thing because I'm sure I heard her say, "Whoa."

"C'mon out, boys," Regina/Doris crooned to them. At first they just sat there in the backseat, looking around like they didn't understand her. "C'mon, c'mon . . ." It was like she was coaxing them. Then she pulled a bag of Chee-tos from her designer purse and waved it at them. They leaped out of the backseat in a way that was so cool, like they were from some Calvin Klein ad. And they were dressed like it, too!

"Isn't this what you girls wanted?" Regina/Doris asked us this question knowing full well that we were having a hard time forming thoughts, much less words. Still, I managed to squeak, "Regina, Doris, whoever, don't say that!" I didn't want these guys to think we were desperate or anything.

"I don't think they understand words," she said, "at least not in the normal sense."

I'm, like, "Huh?"

"What . . . *do* they understand?" Summer asked.

"Chee-tos."

And we're both, like, "Huh?"

"Summer?" It was Judy, Summer's mom. Obviously the situation had changed and a mom was no longer needed. But she was coming, anyway. Calling your mom is like dialing

911. Once you call 911, the police have to come and see if anything is wrong and you can't stop them. "Summer, did you call me?" Judy was answering the 911, and it sounded like she was coming along the side yard to the front.

"Uh . . . I'll . . ." Which is all Summer got out before she sprinted off to intercept her mom.

"They seem really docile to me, so you should be able to handle them," said Regina/Doris. Then she hiked up her tailored skirt and stuck a long, shapely leg into the El Dorado; the rest of her followed. Then she goes, "Here, you're going to need these." And she tossed me the Chee-tos.

Up by the house, Summer had reached Judy and planted herself between her mom and the sidewalk, where the guys were.

"Did you call me?"

Though Summer tried to block her view, Judy noticed right away. "Who are they?"

"Oh, these guys." Summer never lies to her mom and she was okay so far.

Down with the guys who didn't understand words, I had gotten a little more information out of Doris. *"What?!"* Summer heard me and spun around. In fact, the whole neighborhood heard me, probably.

The Cadillac made its usual *chunk* as Regina/Doris pulled it into drive. And I'm going, "Wait, don't go!" But she did.

And like, here's poor Summer with her head swiveling back and forth, wondering what's going on and trying to keep her mom from messing up things, if they had a chance of being good in any way.

I'm still on the sidewalk and I start to back up and the guys start to walk toward me. I didn't get that it was the Cheetos they were after, and why would I at that point? "Summer," I called, "I've really got to see you!"

Summer's doing everything but lying down in front of Judy, who by now thinks she knows what's going on.

"Do I know those boys?" she asked Summer.

"Oh, probably not." Good old Summer, still telling the truth.

"You know we like to meet your friends, Summer. Invite them in and I'll make some lemonade."

Lemonade? Even under normal circumstances that would be humiliating!

And then Judy whispers to Summer something like, "I know what it's like the first time a boy comes over. Don't worry, I'll be cool." Can you imagine how much Summer was dying?

At the same time I'm yelling, "Summm-errrr, gotta tell you something!"

"Just a second, Mom." And Summer runs back down to me and the two cool guys of mystery.

"Who are they?" she whispered as she glanced at them.

"That's what I have to tell you!"

"Where did they come from?"

"A cage! She wasn't kidding about the Cinderella thing, Summer!"

"Hello, boys."

We almost jumped out of our skin. Judy was standing right behind us. She had this friendly smile as she put her arms around us and said, "I'm Judy, Summer's mother."

The guys just looked at her. At the same time, I'm looking at Summer, trying to get her to read my lips.

"And who are you?" asked Judy, giving them her best "welcome aboard" flight attendant smile.

"They're *rats*?!" Summer got it.

"Summer, that's not humorous," said Judy, sort of sternly. Then she turned back to the guys, still waiting for their answer.

"They don't speak," I said, which was true. Then I quickly added, "English." because I didn't want her to start asking questions about handicaps or other disorders.

Then Judy's smile widened. "Are these the foreign exchange students I read about in the paper? The ones from— Sweden?"

Actually, the foreign exchange students were from Spain. But the sprinklers in Summer's yard come on before they get the paper and it gets pretty messed up sometimes. Spain, Sweden, both countries with short names starting with *S*. And the guys were blond (having, only minutes before, been white rats). The important thing is, our hands were clean on this. *We never said they were from Sweden or anywhere.*

"Sweden?" Judy said, and pointed at some imaginary country far, far away. The guys just looked at her. "Sweee-den," she said a little slower and a little louder, like they were developmentally disabled and/or hearing impaired. The guys kept looking blankly at her.

Summer took a breath and I know she was about to blurt out the truth as we knew it at that moment, but she didn't get the chance.

"Sweee-den."

Summer froze with her mouth hanging open. My eyebrows went right to the top of my forehead and became part of my hairline.

It had come from one of the guys that we later figured was probably Scooter because he was always just a little faster to catch on to things. His voice was high and kind of funny, and, I don't know, maybe he sounded Swedish.

"Sweden?" said Judy as she pointed over the top of their heads.

"Sweee-den," said Scooter, and pointed back over the top of Judy's head.

"Of course," she said with a laugh, "it would be more in that direction." Judy had been pointing more toward Louisiana. "Or is it more northeast, which would be that way?" And she points off to the left. So both Spike and Scooter point off to the left. "That's what I thought," said Judy.

Summer was beet red by this time and couldn't stand it anymore. She went right up to the guys and whispered, "Go away! Shoo! Scat!"

"Summer Ann! It's hard enough for them to be in another culture," she said (or species, I thought), "without people being rude."

"You don't understand," said Summer as she turned back to us with a rat boy now on either side of her.

"I understand this," Judy said, putting a friendly arm around me. "They learn about us by the way we act around them."

Spike and Scooter each put an arm around Summer and smiled back at Judy.

Rat Boys

*Q*ll moms are a little different. Jennifer's mother? She's, like, "Sure, go out on all the dates you want with guys who are two years older and have cars. And go see any movie you want, regardless of what they said about it in the Family section of the *Indianapolis News-Press*."

If I said to my mom, "I got asked out by a guy who's on the honor roll, president of the Young Republicans, leads prayer every lunchtime, and promised God to keep his hands to himself," she'd say, "Maybe next year." That's her default answer to everything.

She has rules about everything, even stuff she's never personally experienced or that wasn't even in existence when she was my age. Summer's situation isn't quite as bad. She still has rules and stuff, but her mom gets a little spacey sometimes and forgets the rules and Summer forgets to ask and there you are.

My mom says it's because Judy is extremely busy with her many activities, but I think it might have more to do with an unfortunate decompression event at twenty-two-thousand feet over southern Illinois, when the baggage compartment door blew off her airplane.

She was helping a bunch of businessmen to firmly pull their face masks down to release the flow of oxygen and fit them securely over their mouths and noses because nobody was paying attention when she explained it just before take-off. So she's doing this while heroically ignoring securing her own face mask and, in case you don't know, oxygen is kind of not there at twenty-two-thousand feet.

Nobody was hurt (although lots of luggage fell over southern Illinois and northern Indiana). But if you look at her on the complimentary videocassette they got from CBS News right after it happened, Judy looks a *lit*-tle cross-eyed, if you know what I'm saying.

That being the case, it was lucky that this whole thing happened in front of Summer's house and not mine. My mom is a bookkeeper for Indiana Hydroelectric and knows when something doesn't add up.

The rat boys had zero interest in lemonade. So they just sat at the kitchen table and waited for something else.

"Notice how polite they are?" Judy whispered to us. "They're waiting for you to be seated." We were on the complete opposite side of the room with no plans to get near them. "Sit down, girls," Judy said. "I'll take care of the cookies."

So we sat down on the opposite side of the little table from two guys who were actual rats not more than an hour before and were, I'm sure, totally bewildered. One of them sniffed in our general direction. I took Summer's arm in case she was going to fall onto the floor. I had no idea where her blood sugar was currently at.

"Here you are," said Judy as she put a plate of neatly arranged cookies in the middle of the table. Then she knelt beside us and placed one hand lightly on the table (she never bends from the waist and always holds on with one hand in case of sudden air turbulence). "I'm sure you don't want me hanging around, so I'll be out front. Okay?" She looked at Summer with that same my-baby's-growing-up look that she gave her on the first visit to a doctor that wasn't a pediatrician. "Okay?" she asked again. Summer could only manage a smile.

"Okay," I answered for Summer, who, as I said, wouldn't lie to her mom and who absolutely did not feel that things were okay.

Animals have this zone around them where they feel threatened and Judy was just close enough to the rat boys that she took their minds off the cookies. They watched her and smiled, because she was smiling at them. When she left, it was a different story.

They were used to us from, you know, back at Doris' shop and didn't feel threatened in the least. We had been kind to them and cleaned their cage many times. They looked down at that whole plate of cookies and sniffed again.

"Marci, this is so creepy," Summer whispered. "How can they look so cute and still be rats?" Not the first girl to ask that question, according to *Seventeen*.

The rat boys grabbed for the cookies and started shoving them in their mouths as fast as they could. Summer leaped up from the table and I was right behind her.

"What are we going to do?" Summer said. "I so do not want them in my kitchen! I'm going to have to clean everything they've touched!"

"Oh, come on, Summer, they look pretty clean." And they were, which is what rats are, generally. If you see them in the pet store, they're always washing and grooming themselves. It separates them from other animal life, like Rod & Tod.

Still, I was glad it wasn't my kitchen because in less than a second they had scarfed the cookies and were looking in our general direction. They stood up and started walking toward us and we're all, like, "Eeeek! Eeeeek!" and we ran out of the room, down the hall, and into Summer's room, slamming the door behind us.

It was like some horror movie, where the girls run away to someplace stupid like a room with no other way out and slam the door as if that's going to stop whatever it is that's after them. And then the door gets crashed down or hacked open with a knife and the girls get mutilated. So we waited for the door to get crashed or hacked down and to die from mutilation or from the ant fog, whichever came first.

Nothing happened.

We did hear crashing and banging around, but it was back

down the hall. "The kitchen!!!" screamed Summer. Cleaning the kitchen is her responsibility around the house and she's very protective of it.

Personally, I never eat anything at Summer's house, not since I found out that her dad was working on a formula for fake spit. It's just one of those things that you can't get out of your mind somehow. But it was so clear that not even fake spit would stop two guys who ate James Cunningham's homework three different times!

In the thirty seconds we'd been gone, they had gotten into the refrigerator, where they ate three sticks of margarine, some leftover stroganoff, and a whole package of turkey dogs, including the resealable packaging!

We pushed them away, only to see them go right for the cabinets. All of a sudden it was raining Frosted Flakes, along with raw macaroni and unconverted rice!

I grabbed a box of fish crackers and got their attention. They came at me with this look in their eyes that could have been from one of the more romantically intense episodes of *Dawson's Creek*, but I knew it was more about fish crackers than anything else.

I backed toward the kitchen door, opened it, and tossed the box outside. They went for it and I slammed the door. Summer already had the broom and dustpan. I checked on Judy.

I could see her out the front window, talking to some neighbor, smiling and pointing back toward the house. She had to be talking about Summer's first visit from an actual boy who didn't burp the alphabet.

Summer will make a wonderful homemaker someday because she's very good at it and amazingly quick. This is where I think science genes and flight attendant genes come together the best. By the time I got back, everything was in the trash compactor. All I really had to do was slam cabinet doors shut.

Summer gasped, and I did, too. Spike and Scooter were at the back door. They had finished off the fish crackers *and* the box they came in. Then we heard the front door open. "Summer?" And the guys were pushing their faces against the glass the way they always poked their noses through the bars of the cage when they thought they were going to get something.

We went to the back door and opened it. Summer said, "Shoo!" and I clapped, but they wouldn't be shooed. Like I said, they weren't afraid of us at all.

I grabbed the one we thought was Scooter and Summer grabbed the other one and we pulled them in. We had often held them when they were actual rats and knew that a firm hand would keep them in check.

Judy came in and saw us holding hands with the rat boys. This kind of surprised her.

"I just found out that there are two more exchange students here, from Spain."

"We know about them," said Summer, who had, remarkably, still not told a single lie.

So, there we were, each holding a guy by the arm and standing all close to them and everything. And the guys were smiling, because Judy had inadvertently taught them to do that when she was around. And Summer was all flushed in the face and breathing hard (from having just cleaned a whole kitchen in about seventy seconds). So it totally looked like something was going on, and it was—but not what Judy thought.

"Summer Ann may I see you for a second in the living room?"

I took Spike's arm so Summer could let go. And she went with her mom.

"Summer, these boys might have more advanced attitudes about things. Remember, this is Indiana, not Sweden." And then she's all, like, "I have to go out, and I don't want you and Marci here alone with them. I know what it's like when you're young. Anything can happen and probably will."

And then Judy and Summer came back into the kitchen and Judy was smiling again and goes, "I have to run out for a little while. Here's an idea—why don't I drop you off at the mall, where there are bright lights and about eight thousand people who know you girls and will snitch on you in a second if they see anything going on?"

Okay, I made that last part up, but only because it was what she meant.

Many thoughts passed through our minds on the way to the mall as we sat buckled into the middle seats of the minivan. First and foremost, we thought about the two guys buckled into the seats behind us and what we were going to do with them or vice versa. But we also wondered what a magic ring was doing in Indiana. Not that there isn't a lot of strange stuff in the state.

Doris took us to this rummage sale once where they had an elephant's foot, for crying out loud! And I don't mean a fake elephant's foot, either. It didn't matter that it was a hundred years old. The thought of a three-legged elephant stumbling around Africa was so disturbing, I can't even tell you.

In her shop, Doris also had a deer head on the wall. She got it before we knew her, so we couldn't do anything about that. But we did insist that she pass on the elephant's foot and we also raised her consciousness generally about that kind of stuff. In fact, and this is something Summer and I are proud of, Spike and Scooter were the only animal products to come into the shop after we got there, and they were kept comfortable and healthy if you don't count getting transmutated, which, as far as we could tell, didn't bother them all that much.

But this ring deal—it was way more strange than even an elephant's foot. I think, anyway.

So all this is going through our brains and I'm looking out the window and see HERB IS HANDY on the side of Herb the Handyman's old pickup. I can't say I thought anything about it at the time. I mean, we had these two guys sitting behind us that were actually rats and Judy sitting in front of us trying to teach them English. More about that in a second.

We saw Herb the Handyman one block away from the IGA Foodliner, which is the supermarket Doris goes to, and, if you remember, she said she needed to go to the supermarket. Now, back to us.

"Do-you-have-minivans-in—Sweden?" Judy asked, still

talking really slow, like the difference between English and Swedish was speed.

"They don't understand you, Mom," Summer said, hoping that we could just get there without anything awful happening.

"The fastest way to learn a language is to associate words with objects."

"No, really, Mom. Please? Okay?"

"Summer, I'm just—"

"*Mom!*" Nobody likes to raise their voice, but parents are really bad about not being able to take a hint.

We kind of drove on in silence for a while. Not really silence, Kenny G was coming from the stereo. Judy's got all his CDs, probably because he reminds her of airport waiting rooms.

Then Judy tapped the dashboard and said, "Min-neeee-van." Summer slumped down and put her hands over her eyes. "Min-neee-van," Judy said again.

"Min-neee . . . " came the voice with the funny accent from the one we decided was definitely Scooter.

"Can we just get there, Mom, on account of I'm getting carsick?"

For Summer's sake I tried to act like I didn't think things were going to go nuts at any second. But the truth was, we were both gripping the leather-textured seat handles so hard that the blood circulation to our fingers got cut off.

"Min. Nee."

"Van," said Judy.

"Van," repeated Scooter.

"Min-neee-van."

"Min-neee-van," answered Scooter, a little slower, but still pretty clear, considering.

"I'm really not kidding, Mom!" said Summer. And she was a little green.

By the time we got to Pepper Tree Mall, Scooter had learned four words related to Summer's Voyager, but Spike wasn't talking at all. We didn't know if that was because he was dumber than Scooter or cooler than Scooter (Scooter did sound kind of stupid, nothing against guys from Sweden).

Sometime between when we passed Herb the Handyman's van and when we lost Spike and Scooter at the mall (which is explained in the next chapter), several other things happened. I wasn't there, so I have to guess at this a little.

What I think happened first is that Doris went to the Foodliner. Don't ask me why she would do something like that, because I don't know. She is known as Weird Doris, after all.

If there's no parking at the Foodliner, except for compact spaces, she usually parks just down the street. Her car is seriously not compact.

So she's pushing her shopping cart back to her car, even though you're not supposed to remove the shopping cart from Foodliner property (she does it all the time), and *wah-lah*, she runs into Herb the Handyman. Then she's probably all, like, the same way she was with us. Like, *"Yoo-hoo!"* And, *"Ta-da!!!"* And throwing her arms out and going, "What do you think?"

Well, what *would* Herb the Handyman think? Here's this middle-aged but nonetheless attractive woman with a shopping cart, going up to him and talking to him as if she knows him and stuff.

Herb was probably all, like, "Oh my gosh and golly, why is this sexy babe talking directly to me on account of I'm such a dork that I've been going to ask Doris out since 1973 and haven't so far?" So right away, he's thinking that something's going on.

Now, out of six full-time checkers at the Foodliner, at least one is going to be a serious soap opera freak for sure. And don't forget *Soap Opera Digest*, which is right there at the checkout stands with full-color pictures of you know who, wearing the very same tailored ensemble. So how logical is it that she would be totally recognized? Very, in my opinion.

It's like, once Summer and I saw Tori Spelling in Camden, which is another town close to Indianapolis. And we're going, "Oh my God! Tori Spelling!" and everything. Except, Summer and me asked ourselves, why would Tori Spelling be in Camden, Indiana? It's even more boring than Glenwood. So we decided it wasn't Tori Spelling. I don't think anybody bothered to ask that question about Regina Leigh Savage.

This would explain why the next time I actually saw Regina/Doris, she was on *Glenwood: At Six, on Six* (which is the cheesy cable news on channel six). She was with the mayor, who had named her special guest of honor at the Glenwood Spring Fling because he thought she was Regina Leigh Savage.

I'm not saying Doris lied about who she actually was, but

sometimes you just go with the flow on stuff like this. And if being Regina Leigh Savage means you can get the Mayor to listen to your complaint about basic cable rates when he wouldn't when you were Weird Doris—why not for a little while? Right?

What I know for a fact is that sometime that afternoon, Herb the Handyman called the Glenwood police to report that popular daytime drama star Regina Leigh Savage had murdered Doris Trowbridge at twelve fifty-five that afternoon. He was positive of the time, because it was recorded on, get this, *a videotape that he, Herb the Handyman, had of the actual crime!*

At the Mall

*A*ll right. Yes. We lost Spike and Scooter at the mall. But only for a couple of minutes.

Summer was supposed to be watching them while I called Doris on the pay phone, which I had been doing for about fifteen minutes. She wasn't at Hidden Treasures or at her home. If you don't know why, it means you skipped the last part of the chapter before this.

Like everybody else, Jennifer Martin got out of the old part of town as soon as the parade was over. Most of the people who sponsor the Spring Fling are in the mall, except for The Donut King, who has two locations. Besides being Miss Junior Indiana, Jennifer is the Better Business Boosters' Sweetheart, so she had to boost business at least three hours a week and most of the business was at the mall.

She was at the east entrance of the mall, at Cool Casuals,

where they give her clothes to wear around for free just so she's seen in them. And she's there with Blair and Heather and is probably like, "Can I have some free clothes for my size-five friends, too?" And they probably go, "Yeah, because you're Jennifer Martin."

At the same time, Summer and I were at the west entrance, at the pay phones right by Discount School Clothes That Make You Look Stupid, which is where most of my stuff comes from. I had just left about the tenth message on Doris' answering machine, which, by the way, features Doris imitating Kermit the Frog. It's really annoying, especially in times of crisis.

"Where is she?" Summer demanded, stomping her foot.

"How should *I* know?"

"Let me try," Summer said, as if that was going to make any difference. She grabbed the phone and dug into her pocket for more change.

"Summer!!!" I made her jump and hit herself with the phone receiver.

"Stop shouting my name all the time!"

I had been doing it a lot on that particular day, but this time there was a real good reason to do it. Spike and Scooter had vanished!

"Maybe they turned back into rats," Summer said hopefully.

We looked all around the floor and around the pay phones. Nothing. And also, we hadn't heard any *poof* and Doris said a *poof* always went along with transmutation.

"The food court!" Summer gasped. She sniffed the air and I, too, could smell the aroma of freshly fried burgers.

At the same time, Jennifer, now dressed in a very cool

outfit with white stretch pants, just tight enough to let you know that her mother allows her to wear thong underwear, had moved to the food court herself. She was sitting with Heather and Blair. Each had a number-one combo consisting of fries, medium drink, and a big, big fat cheeseburger. Jennifer can eat stuff like that and never gain weight or get zits.

"Oh . . . my . . . God!" said Blair or Heather. It's sort of like this early-warning alarm thing for Jennifer.

Two of the coolest-looking guys anybody had ever seen anywhere were coming down the escalator and looking right at Jennifer. Kind of.

As she lifted her cheeseburger to her lips, Spike and Scooter gave her a look that said, "Yum, yum!" Jennifer is totally used to that from guys. She casually glanced back at them over the top of her sesame-seed bun.

It's, like, I always thought Jennifer might lose her cheeseburger to a rat. I just never thought I would be the one to stop it from happening.

But we weren't really thinking about Jennifer. We just didn't want the food court turning into a big-budget version of Summer's kitchen.

We grabbed Spike and Scooter just before they got to her and pulled them away. Like I said, they're used to us and never scratched or nipped at us as rats, so they didn't do it as cool guys, either.

So there was Jennifer, watching us lead Spike and Scooter off behind the kiosk that sells imitation designer sunglasses. I wish I had taken the time to see the expression on her face, but we had other things to worry about.

We were holding on to them and trying to figure out what we could do until we found Doris and could get them untransmutated into their former life-forms. Tying them up was too bizarre to think about, especially if somebody came along and saw us doing it. Besides, they would just eat through the knots, anyway.

"Girlfriends! Hi!" We jumped and spun around to see Jennifer walking right up to us with a big friendly smile, like it was such a normal thing for her to be doing that.

"I said to Blair and Heather, 'That looks like Marci Kornbalm and Summer Weingarten,'" she said, while looking at Spike and Scooter. "I thought you might want to sit at our table with us."

"Sit? With you guys?" said Summer.

"God, girlfriend! You act like it's such a big deal." She rolled her eyes and smiled at Spike and Scooter with this look that said, "These poor morons have totally forgotten what very good friends we are." And then she goes, "Yes, of course, sit with us and have something to eat, unless you're not supposed to because of your braces." Sometimes I just wanted to smack her.

Then she goes, "Oh, I'm Jennifer Martin," as if she had just remembered who she was. The rat boys looked at her. So she goes, "And who are you?"

I had this *major epiphany*! It was, like, *ka-boing!!!* Suddenly it was so totally obvious why this was happening to me and Summer.

Jennifer repeats, "Who are you?" Talking to Spike and Scooter like we weren't there anymore.

"These guys," I said. "That we know and you don't."

We were extricated!!! But I only had a second to enjoy it.

"Swee-den."

Oops, I thought.

Scooter pointed toward the food court when he said it. Jennifer's eyes got wide as she looked at us.

"The thing is," said Summer. "These guys are really . . . and it's not our fault, okay? See, what they are is—"

"From Sweden," I interrupted. "That's why we know them and you don't." Which made no sense.

"Sweee-den," said Scooter, and pointed to the food court again.

"Min-neeee-van," said Spike, who picked a fine time to start talking. He also pointed toward the food court.

"That is so cool," said Jennifer. "And you guys are showing them around or something?" Then, with that flirty smile, "What are your names? I hope I can pronounce them." Giggle, giggle.

"Spike and Scooter," I said. "Can you pronounce that?"

"I'm Junior Miss Indiana and also this year's Better Business Boosters' Sweetheart and I am being honored tonight at the Spring Fling dance as well." She left out being Annie three years in a row—probably just ran out of breath.

"All that really means is, I can get you into just about anything, anywhere around here. Would you like to join us?"

She stepped aside and pointed toward the food court, which was all the invitation Spike and Scooter needed. They walked right by her and around the fake imported jewelry kiosk.

She followed them, turning back to us long enough to say, "You guys can take a break; we'll show them around."

What's with that? I thought. I mean, one second we're extricated and the next second we're not?

We looked around the corner of the fake designer sunglasses kiosk. Jennifer was walking up to the table with them and going, "This is Spike and Scooter—they're from Minneeeevan, Sweden. This is Blair and Heather, my two closest friends." Then Scooter goes, "Errr baaag," which they thought was Swedish but was really "air bag." So, Jennifer is like, "Errr baaag," back to them.

Spike reached for a french fry, which they thought was him trying to shake hands. And they kept shaking hands as the guys kept reaching for the fries.

I looked at Summer and I think the same things were going through her head as mine. Logic told us that the rat boys were Jennifer's problem now. But, sorry. This wasn't about logic. This was about guys that belonged to *us*.

"In this country we only shake hands once," Jennifer said to them. Then she noticed us walking up.

"Oh, Marci. Summer. I don't think there's enough chairs for you guys."

"That's okay," I said, as if it totally was okay. "We just wanted to tell Spike and Scooter that we were leaving is all." Then I reached down and got some fries.

"Does my baby want a bite?" Then I leaned in really close to Scooter and fed him a french fry, which he nibbled from my hand. "Yes, he does—he wants a french fry." That's the way Doris talked to them when they were rats, but it takes on a whole new meaning when you're talking to a guy like that. And take my word for it, a guy nibbling something from your hand is a whole different kind of thing from a little furry rodent.

Jennifer couldn't hang on to her smile this time. Though many people had eaten out of her hand, none had done it literally. I handed Summer a french fry for Spike, who then looked at her with that intense fish crackers look.

Summer owned a horse once and knew how to safely hand-feed large animals. So she put the french fry in her flattened palm like she was giving a sugar cube to Audrey's Hope (who was her horse for a while).

Spike ate the french fry right off her palm. Then he licked the palm of her hand. Of course, he was just after the salt and any remaining crumb of french fry, but Jennifer didn't know that. And to Summer's credit, she avoided the "yuck" reflex and managed to act like it happened all the time.

I looked over at Jennifer, Blair, and Heather, and their jaws were almost touching the floor. "Swedish guys," I said. "You gotta love 'em."

Then I get some more french fries and hold them right under Scooter's nose and go, "We're leaving now. You can stay with these guys or come with us. Whatever."

Then I look at Jennifer and go, "Bye, girlfriend," and Summer and I walk away, like we have better things to do. You know?

And the two cutest, coolest guys around stood up and walked away from Jennifer Martin and followed us right up the escalator. How totally utterly great was that?

And I'm holding on to Scooter's arm and Summer's holding on to Spike's arm, because the pretzel place was right at the top of the escalator and we didn't want them running for it. But Jennifer didn't know that. She thought we were holding on to their arms because we were *with* them!

And then we're walking along the upper level, by Hoosier Hits, which is this record store that always has music blasting out into the mall. It was just like being in some movie, walking along with two gorgeous guys with a very cool sound track playing in the background.

And these twelve-year-old girls were looking at us and obviously wanting to be like us. And even some juniors that had never looked twice at us were glancing at us but trying to pretend they weren't!

Then, instead of holding Scooter's arm, I put his arm around my shoulders and put my arm around his waist. So it's like we were walking along and he has his arm around me and I had my arm around him. Then Summer tries it too. I looked back at her and she was fighting off this big grin.

I'm telling you right now, a guy's arm around you feels soooo great! It's Triple Brownie Fudge Overload times twenty, without the calories! Like, your ears get hot. You know? And you can feel different parts of yourself that you don't think about usually, like your fingertips and the backs of your knees. Everything sort of tingles.

Okay, okay. It's not like we forgot that deep down inside, these guys were rats. But I started to think that maybe they could change. I mean, is a rat always going to be a rat no matter what?

I don't exactly know what Jennifer thought after she saw us

glide up the up escalator. Maybe she thought that Spike and Scooter had heard that she already had a boyfriend who was a junior and a JV sprinter and everything. I'm sure she figured out some reason that made sense to her and didn't challenge the laws of the universe as she understood them.

But Jennifer's universe was going to be shaken lots more before the night was over, because right about the same time Spike and Scooter were eating out of our hands, something else was happening a half a block away from the Foodliner.

As would be reported on *Glenwood: At Six, on Six,* later that afternoon, it was there that a crowd had gathered around popular daytime drama star Regina Leigh Savage. Just like I said, a Foodliner checker had recognized her.

And since you can find out everything about anything that happens in Glenwood within two seconds of when it happened, it wasn't too long before the mayor showed up, too.

He probably told her all about the Spring Fling and how it was a nondenominational celebration of springtime in accordance with Supreme Court rulings from the 1970s (it used to be called the Easter Parade and Carnival when Doris was a kid).

Also there, standing in the background (where he lives his life), was Herb the Handyman. He was probably the only person asking a certain question, the same question Summer and I asked about Tori Spelling. "Why is a popular daytime drama star in Glenwood?" But Herb didn't stop there. He asked himself another question. "Why is a popular daytime drama star driving Doris Trowbridge's El Dorado?"

9

The Big Idea

"*Keep them?!*" Summer screeched to a halt in the north entrance parking structure.

We had been walking in the parking structure with Spike and Scooter so they wouldn't smell the food court and also so anybody who saw us with them might think they had a car. Anyway, Summer's, like, "What do you mean, keep them?!"

"Not for *always*. That would be stupid. Probably." I looked at Summer to see if she actually thought it would be stupid and, if she did, how definite she was about it. I got the feeling she was pretty definite.

"Just for tonight is all I'm talking about. What did you think, for crying out loud? After the dance, we send them back to Sweden." That was a metaphor for turning them back into rats, which I didn't want to say out loud because I didn't know how much English Spike and Scooter understood. I gave them each a french fry to take their minds off it, just in case.

"Think about it, Summer. We would have guys way cooler than anybody else, even Jennifer."

Then Summer goes, "You are so obsessed with Jennifer Martin!" How insulting was that?

"I am so *not* obsessed with Jennifer Martin that I can't even believe you said that!"

"You think about her all the time!"

"That's not being obsessed, Summer." I made a mental note to check *Word Wealth* later on for a different word.

"Look," I said as Spike sniffed Summer, which I wish he hadn't done at that moment. "All I want is to go to the dance and not worry about how humiliating it's going to be standing against the wall for three hours instead of dancing our brains out with two cool guys."

"What makes you think they can dance even?!"

"We're gonna teach them," I said, getting all excited about it. "And hey, Summer, you know how good we are. Particularly you, and I mean that, sincerely."

"Yeah, but Marci, they're rats." She was getting a little whiny by then, which is always the signal that Summer's giving in, even if it is against her better judgment.

"You liked the rats in life science. Remember?"

"Yeah, but I never wanted to dance with any of them!" Spike sniffed her again and she pushed him back. "I can so feel my face breaking out over this idea, and I just cleared up."

She *had* cleared up a lot. And because stress is a complexion issue more than anything else, I tried to calm her down.

"It will be easy. All rats really want to do is eat, run on the treadmill, and mate."

"WHAT?!!"

"Which," I added quickly, "doesn't make them much different from most guys. High school guys, anyway." I shoved my last two french fries at Spike because I knew Summer was in no mood to be sniffed anymore.

"So," I said. "We keep feeding them and we exercise them, which dancing is, of course. And that will keep their minds off the mating aspect of the situation."

Spike and Scooter looked at me in a funny kind of way right then. I didn't know what they were actually thinking, but being fresh out of french fries and considering the recent topic of conversation, I thought we better play it safe.

"Maybe you should get a double order of nachos. Extra cheese." Summer didn't have to be asked twice and bolted for the food court.

And so, there I was with them. And there they were with me.

When guys look at you, it can be kinda stupid, or kinda creepy, or kinda fun. It depends on the situation. You know? I was thinking that this was more on the fun side. However, in case I was wrong, I decided to take a big step back and put a fire hydrant between me and them.

They sniffed a little bit, then looked at me again and suddenly, they got a really intense expression. Not fish crackers intense. Like, some other kind of intense.

And I'm suddenly like, *"Whoa!* It's not happening, guys, so just get it off your minds!"

Then I realized that they weren't looking at me. The intense look was for something behind me.

"Hey, it's Marci Cornball!"

It's this name I'd been called since forever, but lately not so much. Only a few boys around still called me that. James Cunningham and a couple of other guys were coming across the parking structure.

"Where's Summer the Spit Princess?" he said, and the other guys laughed. Spike and Scooter made this sound. It was a growl. I sometimes felt like growling at these guys myself, except I never actually did it.

Before I could say anything back to James, Spike and Scooter took off after him. And James is all like, "Whoa, whoa!!!" as they chased him across the garage.

Spike and Scooter were so fast that there was no way he was going to get away. So he jumps onto the roof of this Jeep Cherokee, which makes its car alarm go off. And I'm trying to pull the rat boys away but couldn't!

"Nachos!" said Summer, running up. Thank God there was no line at Taco del Oro.

Summer waved the chips and cheese under their noses and diverted them from James. She led them toward the north entrance door and away from the Jeep Cherokee.

"Who . . . who are they?" James suddenly sounded like he did before his voice changed last year.

"Never mind that, James," I said, talking over the car alarm. "Just take better care of your pets in the future, because you never know what might happen." Then I go, "And don't ever call me or Summer those stupid names anymore."

"Yeah, okay. Whatever," he stuttered as he took another look at the two guys with Summer and me.

I was starting to like this a lot.

Most boys need to be trained to one degree or another. That's not this big put-down; it's just the way it is. When boys are little, their mothers do it. But after a while, their mothers don't have as much control over them as we do. This is because we have something they want (if you don't know what I'm talking about, you'll find out in eighth-grade biology). So it falls upon us girls to make sure they don't go through life eating off the ground, scratching everyplace they itch, and burping the alphabet. I don't want to make too big a deal out of this, but it's pretty clear that the future of civilized society rests on our shoulders. We were lucky with Spike and Scooter, because there were how-to books on the subject.

Rat Training for Dummies was full of a lot of useful information. Like, we found out that Spike and Scooter were fifteen in human years. How perfect was that?! And that they were Russian, but we didn't think that had anything to do with their accents. And that cheese or other milk products isn't really good for them, which made us feel bad about the nachos.

My parents both work and I'm not supposed to have anyone over except for Summer without one of them being there (rule number 1,209). So we took the Glenwood Quarter Bus, which you can ride around Glenwood for a quarter, back to Summer's. However, you're not supposed to have food on the Quarter Bus and the driver caught us opening bags of stuff we got for Spike and Scooter and kicked us off one stop early.

We're walking along with them, heading back to Summer's, and I'm reading, "The best results in training can be achieved through a combination of reward and aversion."

The reward part was easy. Like food, and we stocked up on the way home. Avoiding milk products because of health considerations, we stuck to Chee-tos, Fritos, Pringles, Cornuts, and so forth. But aversion was a different thing altogether.

"That's like punishment," Summer said as she tossed the guys Cornuts one at a time (to keep expenses down). "Suzie's parents talk about it all time because they gotta deal with Harry the beast." Harry is Suzie's brother. He's seven, and he is a beast.

Aversion sounded better than punishment and I can see why they used it in the book instead. Speaking as one who has been punished from time to time, the idea of punishing small animals, even though they were big animals now, kind of put me off. And, like, how would we do it, anyway?

Then I remembered something Rod & Tod got punished for. The Juicer Gooser. It was this random thing they found on the Internet.

When you touched somebody with it, it made this buzz sound and you got a little shock. Not much of a shock, because it ran on AA batteries, but enough to make you jump and enough to make Rod & Tod fall down laughing for about an hour. And enough to get them sent home with a note to their mother that they were never allowed to bring disruptive electronic devices to school again.

Summer stayed out by the sidewalk with Spike and Scooter, because she didn't want to risk getting burped at. Also, neither one of us wanted Spike and Scooter to pick up any bad habits.

Mrs. Cort, Rod & Tod's mother, opened the door.

"Hi," I said. "Is Rod and/or Tod around?"

Mrs. Cort looked desperately tired and old before her time and I felt very bad for her. It looked like she was going to say, "Are you the young woman who will now take over training my boys and help them enter civilized society?" But she didn't and I was glad, because I wasn't feeling *that* bad.

She invited me in, then went out to the backyard to get them. There on the entryway wall was a picture of Rod & Tod when they were, maybe, seven. They were very tidy, their hair combed, faces washed. I remembered them from back then. Me and Summer used to dare each other to kiss one of them. But neither of us ever did, and that's a relief. It would be kind of hard to live with, I mean considering the way they turned out.

"No, you can't bring that in here!" I didn't know what she was yelling about, nor did I want to. "And nobody goes any-where tonight until that room is cleaned up!" Rod & Tod came in, arguing about whose turn it was to clean up their room.

"Hey!" they said.

I was right about Rod, by the way. He hadn't changed since he ran into the trash can a couple of hours earlier. I told them that I needed to borrow that thing the principal took away from them. They looked at me with these grins and Tod goes, "What thing?"

They knew exactly what I was talking about. They just wanted to hear me say it, because it sounded kind of gross.

"That zapper thing," I said. They looked at me. "The Juicer Gooser." I sighed. "Happy now?"

They started laughing and punching each other.

Normally I don't go into boys' bedrooms. My mother doesn't want me to because she says it's not proper. To me, "proper" is a matter of opinion. You know? But disease is disease and a way better reason to stay out of someplace like Rod & Tod's bedroom. They have this ultraserious focus problem, though, so I thought I better stick with them so they didn't get distracted.

Rod poked around under the bottom bunk bed with a yardstick, probably not wanting to put his hand under there. I know I wouldn't.

"It's in here somewhere," Tod said, tossing junk madly around and disturbing the aromatic calm of the atmosphere. I tried not to breathe through my nose because there was serious deterioration going on somewhere in that bedroom.

"Hey," he yelled to Rod, "here's the gym socks I been looking for!"

"You didn't know they were here?" I asked. "Because I could tell right away."

"Yeah? How?" That wasn't a joke. He didn't know.

"Wanna see something we found in the gutter?" Tod had come up with something little that he was holding in his hand. See what I mean about getting distracted?

"No."

"It might be worth something."

"No."

"It was almost going in the storm drain a half block from the Foodliner. I fished it out just in time. See?"

"I don't wanna see anything you found in the gutter, Tod. I know that seems like, so strange to you, but it's just the way I am. What can I say?"

"Hey, Marci," Rod said as he wiped away dust to look out the window. "Who're those guys out there with Summer?"

"These guys we know." Tod came up with the Juicer Gooser. "Thanks," I said. He was still holding the item from the gutter, so I decided to get out before I was grossed out.

"Guys *you guys* know?" Rod didn't ask it like a normal question. There was a definite "I'm so sure" that, while unspoken, hung in the air as if a third gym sock had been discovered.

"What's that supposed to mean?" As if I didn't know. "For your information," I said, "they happen to be our dates for the dance tonight. Feel free to tell everybody you know." I didn't say that last part, but it was okay if they did.

Then they had these smirks all of a sudden. Rod & Tod could be rancorous.

I came down the stairs, stomping loud enough that it alerted Mrs. Cort, who noticed that I was offended. She glared at Rod & Tod as they followed me down, making kissing sounds. Tod still had the thing from the gutter and was probably going to try and put it down my shirt.

"That room has to be cleaned up."

"His turn," said Rod.

"Go!" said their mother.

Tod turned and dragged himself back up the stairs. As he went into his room, he mumbled, "I wish I was in another family."

I heard something just as he slammed the door to his room. It was a *poof.*

You have to understand the context that I heard the *poof* in. There are all kinds of things in the Rod & Tod room that could make a *poof.* For all I knew, it could have been last year's whoopee cushion. Anyway, I didn't think anything of it.

Mrs. Cort glared at Rod, who was following me to the door. "I gotta see these 'dates' you guys got." His mother stopped him.

"I said, you don't go anywhere until your room is cleaned up. Now, go."

Rod turned and headed up the stairs, stomping all the way. This left me alone with poor Mrs. Cort.

"I think it's good that you sent Rod back up," I said, in a very supportive way. "It looked to me like way too big a job for just Tod by himself."

She looked at me in this kind of funny way. Then she goes, "Tod who?"

"Exactly," I said, feeling we had connected on some mutually supporting womanhood kind of level. "Tod who? And for that matter, Rod who, too? Why should I be bothered by their rancorous attitude?"

And she goes, "What?"

I assumed she didn't know the meaning of *rancorous.*

I want you to know that even though March 22 would have turned out way different if I had known what Tod was holding in his hand, it hasn't changed my mind about looking at stuff from the gutter. Even today, knowing what I know, my first reaction would still be, "Buzz off."

Summer's dad was at a saliva convention and his car was in long-term parking at the airport. The Voyager was in the carport. That meant that Summer's garage was totally free. And because it was way in the back of their yard, away from the house, it was the perfect place for everything we had to do.

It took a surprisingly short amount of time to teach Spike and Scooter our dance moves, I mean considering that we had been working on them for three years. Actually, we added some new stuff from MTV earlier that year and changed the middle after we saw *Riverdance*, so it's not like it took us a whole three years to learn one dance. We're not klutzes or anything.

We could have taught it to them quicker even, if Summer's phone hadn't kept ringing. She has a nine-hundred-megahertz, long-range cordless that works all the way to the garage.

The thing is, everybody was so calling us! It's like what I said about how fast people find out stuff in Glenwood.

So Summer's getting these calls about our "dates" and where did we meet them and everything. And Summer says stuff like, "Oh, this friend brought them over." And, "We haven't known them for that long." And, "Sweden was this total misunderstanding; they're really Russians." All very true.

Because the dance stuff was easier than we thought, we

had time left to teach them some stuff to say. They were getting English down pretty good on account of being around us so much.

We stayed with one-syllable words because they turned everything into one-syllable words anyway, like, *Sweee-den* and *min-neeee-van*. That was okay because you can go for a really long time in Glenwood with one-syllable words.

The first phrase we taught them was, "You are so cool." Scooter got it pretty fast and got a whole Twinkie for it. We were going to add, "He is so cool, She is so cool," and "They are so cool." But Spike was a little slower, so we didn't have time. Besides, since they were only going to be talking to us, "You are so cool" was all they needed to know in that regard.

We also taught them, "KIK 105 rocks!!!" That was important because a WKIK-FM guy was going to be at the Spring Fling and if he asks you what WKIK-FM 105 does and you say, "KIK 105 rocks!!!," you win a seven-day trip to Maui. So with Spike and Scooter, we doubled our chances of winning.

They also learned one unfortunate phrase, which I freely admit was my fault. It happened when I accidentally zapped myself with the Juicer Gooser. You know how it is; things slip out. And, because they were single-syllable words, Scooter picked up on it instantly and waited for his Twinkies.

Quick thinking from Summer fixed it. She got Spike to say *bucket* instead. So he's like, "*Ow!* Bucket!" A little unusual, maybe, but socially acceptable.

We only used the Juicer Gooser three times, as it turned out. Twice, if you don't count the time I zapped myself.

Once was when Spike started licking his hands, then rubbing his face, and Summer kind of overreacted. He was just cleaning himself, which is kind of cute when small animals like cats and raccoons do it but kind of gross for a guy. Anyway, Summer was all, like, "Yuck!" Zap.

The second time was when me and Summer were talking about what we were going to wear to the dance. Summer decided on this pink top she had with *Glam* written across it in metal studs, which she bought with some birthday money. It's kind of tight and cut kind of low on top and it's kind of short so her belly button shows.

She had enough birthday money left to get her belly button pierced to go with it. She has an "outie," so it would be very perfect. But Judy said no, and then they had a fight over it and Judy took her to the doctor, who always agrees with whatever our moms say about anything. And of course, the doctor had gross pictures of girls with belly button diseases who probably all live in the same town with the people who have brown teeth with holes in them.

As far as the pink *Glam* top goes, Summer's never really worn it because her mother keeps saying, "That's not appropriate," for wherever it was that Summer happened to be going. However, we both agreed that the dance that night would be highly appropriate.

So as I was saying to Summer, "You look so good in pink," we saw that Scooter (he was more exploratory than Spike) had gotten into automatic transmission fluid that had not been properly stored. I zapped him, but I had to do it. If he had drunk a quart of automatic transmission fluid, it would have probably wrecked everything, not to mention made him sick. As it was, it only wrecked his shirt. Having jumped when he was zapped, automatic transmission fluid splashed down the front.

We could have washed his shirt, but it looked like it was dry-clean only. Then Summer remembered two boxes her mom had stored for Summer's aunt when Steve, Summer's cousin, went into the army. And as I said at the beginning, Steve was this totally way cool dresser.

There were some great shirts packed away and it was easy to pick one out. The next problem was actually taking Scooter's old shirt off and putting the new shirt on. This probably doesn't seem like that big a deal to you, right? Well, excuse me, you weren't there.

"Just unbutton his shirt and take it off, Summer."

"He's yours; you do it." And she was right in a way. Scooter had sort of been mine from the beginning. I mean, he was with me and Spike was with Summer when we were walking through the mall. So that kind of set it up in people's minds. If we switched, there would be a lot of gossip.

Another good reason for me to do it was that Summer was wearing a blouse that also had buttons. And you know, there is the danger of imitative behavior with something like this. I, on the other hand, was layered with two tank tops of complementary colors and zero buttons. Summer stood by, armed with Fritos and the Juicer Gooser, while I undid the buttons on his shirt.

It's like, how many times have you unbuttoned something? About five million? Well, unbuttoning a guy's shirt when the actual guy is in it and watching you while you do it is way different.

I took a quick look. Seven buttons down to his belt and maybe—one more below that.

"Summer," I said. "The shirt we picked out is square cut, right?"

"Uh-huh."

"So . . . it will look cool without having to be tucked in or anything, right?"

"Uh-huh."

Okay. Nothing had to happen below the waistline.

First I had to pull his shirt out from his pants, which was easy enough. I just sort of walked around him and pulled it out in the back, then came back around in front and pulled it out. Then the buttons. I was right, seven, plus one more that had been tucked into his pants.

I started at the top and worked my way down, which is the way I usually do buttons. And I'm thinking, God, I hope he doesn't have a lot of hair, and if he does, don't make it rat hair. I mean, they looked like these cool guys that were maybe in a band or something, but that was with clothes on. Who knew what the rest of them looked like?

One button, then the next, then the next, and so forth. And then his shirt was open all the way down.

His skin was really smooth, what I could see of it. So I stopped worrying about rat hair.

"God, Marci!" Summer whispered. "Take a picture, why don't you?" And maybe I wasn't doing this really fast, fast enough for Summer, anyway. It's just that my ears were kind of warm again, and for a split second, I forgot how to breathe, weird as that sounds.

After the buttons, taking his shirt off was a bigger deal than I thought it would be. I mean, I could have gone behind him, grabbed ahold of the collar, and kind of yanked it off, I guess. But I wanted to be sort of gentle about this. We had always been gentle with them as rats. You know? So I reached inside the front of his shirt and pulled his left arm back out.

He had muscles. Not the big, gross, WWF kind. But I could feel them and his arms were solid, not like mine or Summer's at all.

So then, with one arm out, it was easy to slip the shirt off the other arm. "Summer, feel this," I said, touching Scooter's arms again.

"No-wah! God!"

"Summer, it's not like they aren't used to us holding them and petting them."

"When they were rats! And when they were rats, you were hardly interested in them at all!" I didn't get her point, exactly.

"Just feel this."

Summer took a step closer and gave Scooter some Fritos. Then she ran her hand across the upper part of his arm. Everything was silent for a second. Summer had forgotten how to breathe too.

"Summer? Are you in the garage?"

We both jumped. It was Summer's mom, and there we were in the garage, with two guys and one without a shirt!

Nocturnal Animals

It turned out that Judy wanted the cordless phone, is all. Summer caught her in the backyard, before she got to the garage, and gave it to her while I was putting a clean shirt on Scooter. I have to admit that I was a lot quicker getting a shirt back on him than I was taking the shirt off him, but that's panic for you.

"What have you girls been doing in the garage all this time?" Judy asked. I am sure that Summer was blushing beyond belief. But like I said, blondes like Summer turn different colors really easy and most of the time it doesn't mean anything's going on.

"Were you practicing for the dance tonight?" Judy asked.

"Mostly," Summer answered.

"Well, you better take a break because it looks to me like

you're getting overheated. We don't want you fainting again." And she turned and went back to the house.

So while we were admiring Scooter, and then while Summer was outside giving the cordless phone back to Judy and I was doing up buttons faster than I had ever done buttons in my life, nobody was watching Spike.

This could have been very serious because, besides improperly stored automatic transmission fluid, there were all kinds of other common household hazards in the garage. We were lucky because all Spike did was curl up on some old carpet samples and go to sleep. When we remembered him and checked, he was out like a light.

Summer thought the worst had happened and that Spike was, in fact, the tragic victim of detergent or drain declogger intake. This is because she had a hamster die on her once when she was six for like, no reason.

"Summer, he's just sleeping," I said.

"That's what my dad said about Mickey," she answered. Mickey was the deceased hamster (when Summer first got him, she thought he was a mouse).

"Look," I said, referring to *Rat Training for Dummies* and whispering so we wouldn't wake Spike up. "They are nocturnal animals, right? They've been awake all afternoon, learned a whole dance and sixteen monosyllabic words, and all that after going through cross-species transmutation. Who wouldn't be wiped out, for crying out loud?"

Then Scooter came over and curled up beside Spike, which is the way they usually slept in the cage. Once again, things were working out so perfect. We quietly removed all the household hazards we could find and carried them out to the side of Summer's house, then closed the side door to the garage.

Summer can see the garage from her bedroom, so it was easy for her to keep an eye on things while she got ready. We put new AA batteries in the Juicer Gooser just to make sure. Plus she had a whole box of Ding Dongs that we hadn't even opened yet, so she was pretty well prepared. My number was on the speed dial just in case.

My mom was already home and my dad was just pulling into the driveway when I got there. Back then, my dad was on this kick about how we didn't talk enough, so there was a possibility that he might want to have a meaningful dialogue about my day.

It used to be that he would go, "How was your day?" And I would go, "Okay," And that was that. Then he and my mom were at this school meeting where a shrink from I. U. was all, like, "Not talking to your kids is the cause of everything that's wrong with the world." Now he wants details on how my day was, like I'm supposed to be taking notes or something all the time.

I know my parents pretty well and I just felt that there was probably a rule that covered transmutation, like "no dating until you're sixteen and that includes any guy who was recently another life-form." So it was wise to avoid any discussion that included details about my day.

I got to the front door at the same time as my dad and we went inside together.

"Hi, Daddy! How was your day?"

"All right," he said. "How was your day?"

"Great!" I said, like I was bubbling over with excitement, which I was.

"That's nice."

End of dialogue.

While it's true that my dad wants us to talk more, he only wants to when he thinks I don't. If he thinks I want to talk, he's afraid I'll talk his leg off and bails at the first opportunity.

"How was your day?" Mom asked.

"Great," I said.

Same thing with Mom.

Kiss, kiss, and I'm off to the shower with some routine information yelled back and forth as I go down the hall.

"Did you go to the orthodontist's?"

"Yeah."

"Did he say anything?"

"Brush better."

"Anything else?"

"No."

"That's good."

I started with a nice long shower even though my mom gets on my case for wasting hot water. I didn't want to make her mad or anything, but I just felt like I had to stand under the shower and rehearse some of the stuff I might need to say that night. Like, "Well, we're not really going together; I'm still thinking it over." Stuff like that. It was so cool to be able to practice things like that and know I was going to be saying it for real, and maybe more than that! Maybe, like . . .

"KIK one-oh-five rocks!"

"We have a winner!!!"

"You mean we won the trip to Maui?!!!"

"Do you think you and Summer will be taking your dates to Maui, Marci?"

"Of course we will!"

"Well, Marci and Summer, there are lots of girls that would love to be you tonight."

"Really? Like who?"

"Like Jennifer Martin!"

"Oh, yes, I think I remember her."

"Marci, please take me to Maui with you and Summer and your dates. I never meant any of the dirty looks I always gave you and the things I said about you ever since the second grade!"

"Please don't beg, Jennifer. It's better if you stay here and be Miss Junior Indiana while we're in Maui!!!"

Then the hot water was all gone and I got out of the shower. It's really hard to practice saying stuff in cold water.

I figured I had about fifteen minutes of hair drying and makeup and then last-minute hairstyling and details.

First the base to hide those little flaws of natural skin tone, then the shadow, liner to accentuate (this is tricky because liner goes in and out of style almost every year), and finally blush, which I'm very careful with, especially when I might be headed for a major blushing situation. I always advise Summer to stay away from blush altogether.

My mom came into the bathroom right between liner and blush and started yelling at me. I mean, she had to yell at me because I had my headphones on and I couldn't hear her. As far as I knew at that moment, I wasn't in any trouble.

"Yeah, Mom?" I said, pulling a headphone away from my ear.

"Your father and I need to speak with you."

Uh-oh! My brain raced. Maybe it was just usual stuff.

"It's not too much makeup, Mom!"

"Yes, it is, but that's another subject. Come on."

"This skirt isn't too short—everybody dresses this way."

"Will you come on, please?"

Uh-oh! Not the makeup, not the skirt. There was no rule about hair that I knew about. That didn't leave too much else.

"Did (gulp) Summer call?" I waited for it to hit the fan.

"About what?

"Nothing." Phew!!! What, then?

The TV was on in the living room when I got there, the cheesy cable news show *At Six, on Six.* There on the screen was the incredible simulation of Regina Leigh Savage! She was surrounded by a crowd and was standing with Mayor Ed Field, who is known as either Mayor Ed when he's the mayor or Smilin' Ed when he does cable commercials for his hardware store.

"Ms. Savage has agreed to be our guest of honor tonight at the kickoff of Glenwood's annual and nondenominational Spring Fling." And the simulated Regina Leigh Savage was saying, "I'm so thrilled to be here in Glenwood." And now she sounded half like Doris and half like Monica on *Carlton Plaza.*

And then the TV guy is going, "The popular daytime

drama star was spotted at the IGA Foodliner here in Glenwood, which is rated number one in freshness, quality, and customer satisfaction." And in the background I saw Herb the Handyman saying, "Ask her why . . . Why is she—" But he never got to finish his question, because there was a cut. Then Herb was gone and it was just the mayor and simulated Regina Leigh on TV.

But I couldn't really listen, because my dad started talking the second I got into the room and Mom shut the TV off. "Marci, you know Herb. He's worked here before." Herb the Handyman was standing in the living room! He was looking at me funny and he had a shoe box under his arm.

"Oh," I said, hoping for the best. "I didn't put a fork down the garbage disposal. Can I go now?"

Then Officer Henderson stepped into the room from the kitchen, where he had been talking on the phone. I knew him from fifth grade, when he talked to our class about bicycle safety.

"Well," I said. "I don't ride my bicycle anymore. Can I go now?"

"Marci," said Officer Henderson. "Herb believes that something has happened to Doris Trowbridge and he believes you know something about it."

"Well . . . you know . . . like, lots of stuff happens and it's kind of hard to keep track all the time. Can I go now?"

"This is serious, Marci," my dad said. And I knew it was, because they kept using my name in every sentence.

"Marci," said Officer Henderson. "Herb thinks that this television actress has assaulted Doris—"

"Shot her!" said Herb. Herb has a stutter, by the way. I won't imitate it here, because that would be cruel. But it did take him a while to get "shot her" out.

"Now, Herb," said Officer Henderson. "We don't know that."

"It's on the videotape," Herb said, taking a long time to get it out. He sort of waved the shoe box around while he was saying it. "You hear that actress threaten her, Doris stands up, and the gun shoots, you hear it shoot, and Doris falls down. It's all right here." And then he goes, "You were on the tape, too." Then Officer Henderson took the shoe box from Herb.

"Herb went to Hidden Treasures to check on Ms. Trowbridge. The door was unlocked, even though she wasn't there."

"She has short-term memory loss," I said, trying to cooperate. "Can I go now?"

"Marci," he continued, totally not appreciating my cooperation. "An old video camera was sitting on a counter and it was in the recording mode."

Eeek and a half! It was so possible!

I remembered Doris going, "On, off, on, off, on," when she was showing us how good her eyes were, then she took a video of me and Summer, then she put the camcorder down to show us the ring, but I never heard her say "off," so it could have been recording the whole time. How *Blair Witch Project* was that?!

"Herb put the cassette in a VCR at Hidden Treasures and viewed it," explained Officer Henderson. "Unfortunately, the cassette was ruined in the viewing process." And he pulled around eight miles of wrinkled videotape out of the shoe box. A dead cassette dangled from the end of it.

"But I saw enough, before it jammed," Herb stuttered.

"What we want to know, Marci," said Officer Henderson while holding the twisted tape and dangling the dead cassette, "is can you explain what happened here?"

"Yes, I can. The VCR at Hidden Treasures is really old and it eats tape all the time. You have to be careful to put the cassette in straight, or it will—"

"Marci," he said, totally interrupting me. "That's not what we wanted you to explain."

"Oh. What, then?"

And my mom goes, "Can you excuse us a second?" And she drags me off to the kitchen and closes the sliding door.

"Marci Katlin," my mom says, using my first and middle names in the sentence so I know it's *very* important. "Herb is talking about somebody being murdered. The police don't really think anything happened, but they would like you to tell them what you know."

So, okay. What can you do in a situation like this? I go, "Mom, I don't know exactly what happened on account of I wasn't there."

"So you're saying that something *did* happen?"

"Well, of course something happened, Mom. Something always happens in life."

And she goes, "Could we can the philosophy and stick to the point?" It is so like my mom to think that life is not the point.

With the sliding door shut and her leaning against it with

her arms folded, I really had no choice. I told her what I thought *might* have happened.

"The camcorder was pointing at the back room, where Doris was watching the climactic Friday installment of *Carlton Plaza*. Then Doris got this idea about something that I would prefer not to go into at this time and stood up. Right at that instant, Monica shoots George, which is exactly when Doris fell over the rat cage I had left in her way. On tape it might have looked like she was shot, but she just tripped."

Having explained everything to my satisfaction, I said, "Can I go now?" And she's like, "*May* I go now." Okay. "May I go now?" And she goes, "No, you may not." Grammar lessons that lead nowhere are such a total waste of time.

"Herb said he heard somebody on the videotape threatening Doris."

"That was Monica threatening George on *Carlton Plaza*. Duh."

"Don't give me that attitude, young lady!"

And I go, "What attitude? I'm just telling you what I think happened, for crying out loud! *May* I go now?"

"You're grounded."

I told her what happened, I used correct grammar, and I still get grounded! How random is that?!

"You are in your room until you can tell us what you know about this and without the attitude."

I really, really don't get stuff like this. It's like, every time I show any kind of emotion at all or express any kind of opinion at all, they go off about my *attitude*! As if my mom wasn't totally bellicose herself a lot of times!

Stomp, stomp, stomp, slam, flop (on my bed).

So there I was. No dance. No dates. No Maui. And then I'm thinking, No way!

I had only ever sneaked out twice in my whole life, but only got caught once. It's not something I'm proud of, and I only did it because I had to. This was another time that I had to. And because, as far as they knew, it would only be my *second* time (if I got caught), I probably wouldn't be facing Westerly Academy for Girls, which is a boarding school in Camden and the ultimate aversion threat in our house.

First I did some whining, real loud. Stuff like, "This is so unfair! Nobody ever gets punished like this for no reason." This is so my parents would know that I was in my room and not liking it. If you get sent to your room and you're all like, "I don't care, I want to be in my room, I'm happy," they get madder and come in and yell at you some more. So it has to sound like you're all bummed out and learning a lesson. Not too loud, though, because then they come in and yell at you about that.

Usually they'll come in after they think you've had time to consider how totally wrong you were. But, and Summer and I figured this out, they won't come in if they think you're asleep. It's like, "Let her sleep; it's probably just PMS."

Then what you need is a body for the bed, so when they peek in (hopefully not until it's dark), they see something. I have a great stuffed Raggedy Ann that I won two years ago at the Spring Fling. It's the only thing from my childhood that I've kept, and that's only because it's pretty big and has a head almost the same size as mine, so when the covers are pulled up, it looks like I'm there.

Summer and I made this great tape, just in case we needed it. It's snoring and sleeping noises. It's really good and my boom box has "stereo surround," which makes it sound real. I hid it under my bed so the sleeping sounds came from the right direction.

I had my purse in my bedroom, with my lip gloss and brush, so I was pretty set for the dance. Money was a problem, so I had to take my four Susan B. Anthony dollar coins that my grandparents gave me as souvenirs of the twentieth century.

I stomped around and whined about how other kids never got punished like this for about ten minutes. Then I listened. The TV was back on. A good sign.

I heard my mom say, "Maybe she just needs to get some sleep." A very good sign. I started the sleep noise tape and went for the window.

The last two times I went out the window, it was easy. This time the bougainvillea was in bloom and growing all over that side of the house. It's got thorns, which I didn't think about until I was halfway out. The other times I had jeans on, too.

So there I was, dangling in a skirt, which got caught on thorns and was sliding up while I was sliding down. And I'm trying to keep my legs away from the bougainvillea so I don't get scratched up and look like I was attacked by Freddy Krueger on the way to the dance.

Then I remembered that the sprinklers come on at six-thirty because we never water during the heat of the day. We're very sensitive to resource usage because of my mom's job with Indiana Hydroelectric. I couldn't see my watch on account of holding on to the windowsill, but it had to be close to six-thirty.

I hadn't been scratched yet, but my underpants were now showing and I was about to be watered. I let go.

I stood up, pulled my skirt down, and checked everything I could see on myself. I was okay so far. I turned to leave and bumped right into Doris as Regina Leigh Savage. I almost screamed.

"Shhh," she said. "Somebody will hear you."

"You're telling me?"

"Everybody thinks I'm Regina Leigh Savage," she said as she pulled off her stylish high heels and rubbed her feet.

"Just a guess," I said. "But maybe it's because you're telling everybody you are."

"Yeah, well," said Doris as Regina Leigh, "fame is intoxicating. One good thing, your basic cable rate will be lower, starting next month. And you can put out two extra trash barrels for pickup without being charged an additional fee by the city." As it turned out, Doris as Regina Leigh had spent most of the afternoon with the city council, making up for all the times they didn't listen to her when she was Weird Doris.

"Look, Doris," I said. "The sprinklers are going to come on any second and I can't even tell you what will happen to my hair if it gets wet."

"What were the police doing here?"

"Herb the Handyman thinks you murdered yourself."

"What?!"

Suddenly I'm shhhing her.

"But I'm not murdered! I'll just show him." And I go, "Looked in the mirror lately?" And she's, like, "Oh, yeah."

"You're in this mess, Doris," I said, keeping an eye on the Rainbirds, "because you're trying to be something you're not. And you lied just so everyone would think you were this really important person."

"It was nice to have people be idolatrous," she said, wistfully using her improved vocabulary.

"My advice," I offered as I applied lip gloss, "is use the ring to turn yourself into yourself and then be the best that you can be. And also show Herb the Handyman that you aren't murdered."

"The ring! That's why I came over here."

"Seriously, Doris. We have to get off the lawn, now."

"I lost it."

The Rainbirds came on. I'm suddenly running along the side yard with a simulated popular daytime drama star, trying to keep my hair dry and yelling, "WHAT DO YOU MEAN, YOU LOST IT?"

11

Betrayed

$\mathcal{T}$here is a gate in our rear fence that opens to the yard behind us, which belongs to the Kochendorfers. So we're running along the Kochendorfers' side yard, which puts us onto the street around the block from my house. As we're going, Doris was telling me what she thought happened.

The ring was probably a size six and Doris's finger was a size seven when she was Doris, but a size five when she became Regina Leigh Savage. It made sense that it could have slipped off, especially if she was *"ta-da*ing" all over the place like she had been doing at Summer's.

"It has to be in my car or at my shop," she said. "Or maybe at the supermarket, because I was there, too."

"My stars and garters!" This was said by Mrs. Kochendorfer, who says this about anything that happens in her life. She was saying it now because Regina Leigh Savage was standing in front of her house. "It really *is* you! I saw you on *Rosie O'Donnell* this afternoon and then on *Glenwood: At Six, on Six* right after! And now here on my sidewalk!" And her screen door slammed as she disappeared back into her house.

"Great," I said, wondering how long it would take for everyone to know I wasn't in my room anymore.

"*I was on* Rosie O'Donnell?" asked Doris, who was suddenly worried that her short-term memory loss had gotten worse. I explained that the real Regina Leigh must have been on *Rosie O'Donnell* while Doris was on Glenwood's cheapoid cable news. Things were starting to get confusing.

"Marci," she said, "I need your help! I'll look for the ring in my car and at my shop. You take the supermarket. Okay?"

"Doris, I'm grounded! I'm not supposed to go *anywhere*!"

"You said you were going to the dance."

"*That's the whole point!!!*" I was getting really frustrated about how nobody ever got the point. "I sneaked out and now Mrs. Kochendorfer saw me and I am going to be in so much trouble I can't even tell you. And if I'm going to be in that much trouble, I wanna be in it for going to the dance, not for going to the Foodliner!"

Mrs. Kochendorfer came running back out with a pencil and paper and said, "Can I have your autograph? 'Best wishes to Grace.'" And Doris as Regina was signing this autograph while she's going, "Marci, please. Please."

"Okay, okay! I'll check at the supermarket!"

"Thank you, Marci," she said as she handed the autograph to Mrs. Kochendorfer. "I know it's a sacrifice for you."

"You misspelled 'Regina,'" said Mrs. Kochendorfer.

"Oh, I'm sorry," said the simulated Regina Leigh Savage as she corrected it.

Things were calmer at Summer's. But that was about to change, too.

After she had done her hair and makeup and gotten ready in her outfit with the pink *Glam* top, she went out to the garage to get Spike and Scooter so they'd all be ready to take the Quarter Bus to the dance when I got there. As I suspected she would, she had abandoned the twin ponytails. Her hair was now down in this kind of a Michelle Williams from *Dawson's Creek* thing, which, along with her figure, made her look older, like at least eleventh grade.

Summer had also been practicing stuff to say when we were surrounded by the curious and the envious. Unlike I, however, who concentrated on Maui, Summer had worked on some explanations in case Spike said, "Ow, bucket," at a time when it didn't fit the conversation.

Practicing some dance steps as she went, Summer crossed her backyard carrying a fresh box of Ding Dongs and the garage door opener. She pressed the button. The door went up.

"Eeek!" Summer said, and then, "Oh, no!"

Spike and Scooter had learned more than we thought. They had gotten into Steve's clothes and not only had the ability to do buttons, but zippers and belts. The fact that they had put on Steve's clothes instead of eating Steve's clothes proved that things were starting to spin out of control. Plus they looked very cool for having made their own fashion choices.

"You look so good in pink," Spike said, and for just a second, Summer got all flattered and was, like, "Really?"

Then she remembered that basically, she was talking to a rat who was just saying what he thought would get him a reward. And besides, Steve's clothes were tossed all over the garage and Summer didn't want them to get messed up or her mother to find out.

So Summer started stuffing the clothes that Spike and Scooter hadn't selected back into the boxes. And she was bending down to pick them up from the floor when she got this uneasy sexual harassment feeling and saw the rat boys looking at her.

It was unclear if they were looking at her cleavage or her belly button or just her Ding Dongs, but Summer wasn't taking any chances. So she assumed a confident, assertive stance and forcefully said, *"No!"* Which is this whole YWCA thing we learned last year.

"No!" Scooter forcefully said back to her, which was a little scary.

So adding to what we learned at the Y, Summer forcefully said, "No!" again, but this time thrust the box of Ding Dongs out in front of herself, like a shield of armor.

"Yo. Ding Dongs," said Scooter.

This was very disturbing to Summer because we never taught them to say "Ding Dongs." And she had no idea where they picked up "yo" because, as an everyday expression, it is not in our lexicon.

"Summer!" Judy was calling down from the house. "You have a visitor."

Summer thought it was me, so she jiggled the box at them to focus their attention and lead them out of the garage. But it wasn't me at all.

"We are so proud of you for winning Junior Miss Indiana, Jennifer," said Judy, as if she was going to offer Jennifer a pillow and headphones.

"I know," replied Jennifer. "Everybody is."

Summer was busy pulling on a sweater so her mom wouldn't notice the pink *Glam* top and, at the same time, trying to keep the rat boys under control as she came in the back door.

"Girlfriend, hi!" Summer jumped when she heard the voice.

"Errr baaag," said Jennifer, giving the new traditional Swedish greeting.

"Errr baaag," replied Spike and Scooter.

"Oh," said Judy turning around to see them. "The boys are back?"

Poor Summer. This was too much for her to handle by herself. I should have been there. But you have to give her credit on account of she still stuck to the truth.

"Marci and I were taking them to the dance."

"Too bad about Marci," said Jennifer, as if she cared at all. "I was just over at her house and her mother told me she was grounded and had gone to bed and was fast asleep. So I said to myself, why don't I see if Summer and the boys need a ride, I mean, if the boys were here, of course."

"Well, I don't know," said Judy. "Are your parents driving?"

"Randy Frasier is driving. He's a junior and very responsible. And, as he's my former boyfriend, I can vouch for him."

Summer's now, like, completely confused and goes, "When did you and Randy break up?"

"Sometime tonight. I haven't decided when yet. Shall we go?"

"You are so obsessed with Jennifer Martin," said Scooter, hoping for a Ding Dong.

"I guess that's a yes." Jennifer beamed, then reassured Judy. "Don't worry, Mrs. Weingarten. I get that all time."

Going to the Foodliner made me late. But I had promised Doris I would look for the ring and I was going to do it, no matter how much I wanted to get to the dance.

So I run up to the general night manager and ask, "Did any of you guys find a ring around here?" And he goes, "No." And I'm, like, "Thanks, bye."

I made a quick stop to call Summer and tell her that I was on the way. But her mom said that she already left. I thought that she probably got nervous keeping Spike and Scooter in the garage and had hopped on the Quarter Bus.

I'm generally pretty good with budgeting my time and I calculated that I had about an hour to be cool at the dance with Spike, Scooter, and Summer, then figure out someplace to store them for the night and get back home. It all seemed pretty doable to me. I would probably get busted sometime the next day, whenever my mom stumbled across Mrs. Kochendorfer, but that was tomorrow and this was tonight.

* * *

Rod or Tod was standing with some other guys by the entrance to the Kickapoo Pavilion, burping the alphabet. It's funny, I had never seen them apart or even thought of them as two people all that much. They were always together, "Rod & Tod, the dorkmeister twins." You could sort of tell them apart on a day-to-day basis according to the individualized stains. But seeing one alone was kind of weird. He was only able to burp down to *H,* so it was probably Rod.

"So where's your hot 'date'?" Then he smirked and added, "In your dreams?"

"Where's your brother?" I replied. "Home pretending to take a bath?"

I handed two Susan B. Anthony dollars to the ladies at the card table by the front entrance and got my ticket. One of the ladies said she was going to hang on to the Susan B. Anthony dollars and give them to her grandson. There's probably about two billion Susan B. Anthony dollars in the sock drawers of grandchildren across America.

When I got inside, the dance was going great. The band was The Beatles Experience, from Bloomington. They dressed like the Beatles and did all the Beatles stuff exactly the way you hear it on oldies radio, except there was no "Ringo." Instead there's a guy on keyboards who did all the drum stuff with a synthesizer, plus other instruments that were on the records back then.

Because the dance is open to everybody over twelve, including adults, they usually get bands like that instead of something like "Nine Inch Nails Experience." It's okay because, after about an hour, they start playing stuff from the current millennium and are pretty good at doing it just like the CDs, which Summer and I prefer.

So I'm walking in and the band is playing "Yellow Submarine," which you can't really dance to but everybody likes anyway. And everybody was singing the chorus, "We all live in a yellow submarine," and whistling and clapping (big fun in Glenwood), and I was walking to the beat and being all like, cool and looking around for my best friend and our dates. Then I see another weird thing.

The first weird thing had been Rod without Tod. The second was Heather and Blair without Jennifer, to whom they had been stapled since second grade.

I'm thinking, Nuts! Jennifer's not here to see me and Summer with our dates! Then I'm like, Wait a minute, why aren't Heather and Blair with Jennifer, wherever she is? I mean, even if she was in the rest room, they'd be right there with her.

I couldn't hear that well because of "Yellow Submarine," but I heard them say something about, "If she thinks (something) she is (something, something) and a total witch, anyway." But because it wasn't Halloween, I don't think they said "witch," exactly.

"HI!" I said, talking loud enough to be heard over "Yellow Submarine." I smiled at them as if it was normal for me to say hi and smile at them. "SO, WHERE'S JENNIFER?"

"WE DON'T KNOW AND WE DON'T CARE!"

This is so startling that I'm like, "WHOA! WHAT HAPPENED?"

"SHE BLEW US OFF JUST BECAUSE SHE FOUND SOME-BODY ELSE SHE LIKES BETTER!" That was Blair who said that. Then Heather goes, "SUDDENLY SHE ACTS LIKE WE'RE NOT WORTHY OF HER FRIENDSHIP!"

Deep down inside I was thinking, You got what you deserved, you little suck-ups. But I always let bygones be bygones and offered them some heartfelt advice, which was hard to do because I had to scream it over the music.

"GUYS, JENNIFER WAS NEVER REALLY YOUR FRIEND. OKAY? A REAL FRIEND IS SOMEBODY WHO IS THERE FOR YOU NO MATTER WHAT. SOMEBODY WHO WILL NEVER ABANDON YOU JUST BECAUSE SOMEBODY ELSE COMES ALONG THAT SHE'D RATHER BE WITH. A REAL FRIEND DOESN'T . . . do . . . that. . . ." I kind of stopped with my mouth hanging open, because I saw something I thought I would never see in my whole life.

It was Summer, my best friend in life, and she was standing with Jennifer Martin! Not only standing with Jennifer, but talking with Jennifer and laughing with Jennifer!!!

This was no longer my best friend since forever standing there. No, no. This was some stranger I hardly knew, in a stupid pink *Glam* top that showed off how developed she was compared to me and wearing platform shoes as if she wasn't way taller than me, anyway!

She was holding hands with Spike and Jennifer was holding hands with Scooter! And everybody thought it was so cute the way the rat boys ate cookies right out of Summer's and Jennifer's hands.

I don't want to make too big a thing out of this, so I'll just say that I was totally, utterly, and in the most heinous way possible, *betrayed*. And bad as that was, it got even badder.

The Beatles Experience ended "Yellow Submarine" and started "Twist and Shout," which is a song everybody can dance to. And I had to stand there, against the wall where I had been for the last two years of my life, and watch Summer and Spike and Jennifer and Scooter dance. Not just dance, but, like, dance right in the middle of the Kickapoo Pavilion, where the spotlights all come together! And they were dancing the dance Summer and I had worked on since the sixth grade! And this circle of people formed around them, and everybody was watching them because they were so good.

Right when it was hitting me just how deep this wound was and how much it was going to affect my entire life from that point forward, Rod comes up and says, "What did you mean about my brother?"

"Will you be quiet!" I said. "I'm trying to think!"

And I thought about how devastatingly tragic my life had become in such a short—

"Was it supposed to be a joke?" asked Rod, rudely interrupting my dark reflections again.

"Yes, it was a joke. I'm sure he really takes a bath sometimes. Now beat it, I'm busy!"

And I felt myself plunging into a black pit of despair that only—

"See, I don't get that."

"GET WHAT?" I yelled, which Summer heard and looked over at me while Rod goes, "The bathing brother thing."

"MARCI!!!" she screamed, as if she was sooo happy to see

me and didn't know how deep the wound was that I was thinking about before Rod interrupted me.

Summer's running over to me and I say, *"I so hope you are totally satisfied, Summer!!!"*

"If it was supposed to be some kind of burn," Rod babbled, "you gotta explain it, because I don't feel all that burned."

"I was talking about Tod, Rod, and how you're always together and now you're not. Okay? Bye." Then I turned back to Summer and go, "It looks like you're having a great time with *your new best friend*! Sorry I barged in!!!"

"Jennifer said you were grounded," Summer said, like there was some kind of misunderstanding, even though it was totally obvious what was going on.

"And you were just sooo quick to believe Jennifer, right?"

"You weren't grounded?"

"Yes, I was grounded! But that's so not the point!"

"Who's Tod?" asked Rod.

"Your brother, Rod! *Tod!*"

"I don't have a brother," he said with that smirk.

"Perfect," I replied to Rod. "You turn against the one person in life who is like a brother to you because he is!" Then I looked right at Summer and go, "You two have a lot in common when it comes to turning against people." And Summer's like, "Huh?" as if not getting the point.

Then Mayor Ed walked up between us and called to Jennifer while I was trying to make Summer get the point. "Jennifer, I need to see you a second," he said.

"The point is, Summer," I said, now having to look around

Mayor Ed. "While you and Jennifer were here, having such a great time with your dates and being blondes together and everything—"

"Hi, Mayor Ed," said Jennifer, not caring that she had also stepped between us and I couldn't see Summer at all anymore.

"Let's step over here where we can talk for a second." And Mayor Ed walked Jennifer away.

"While you were here, treading asunder our so-called friendship, Doris was in desperate need of our help! *Desperate*, Okay? I and I alone was the only one of the two of us that was there for her in her time of need, because one of us in a pink *Glam* top was more interested in herself at that moment in time, I guess! How bad do you feel now?!"

"Doris is in trouble or something?" Summer asked.

"THAT'S NOT THE POINT AND YOU KNOW IT!" I yelled. "The point is that I always thought that you really, actually *did* want to sit with Jennifer at her birthday party that time and leave me alone with Rod & Tod. Something that I spent endless hours hoping wasn't true but now I know totally was and I am wounded beyond belief!!!"

"Tod who?" said Rod, still hanging around.

"This is a private conversation," I said to him, "so go find a whoopee cushion and sit on it!"

"You think I was with Jennifer because I wanted to be, instead of with you?" asked Summer.

"Duh! Why would I think that? Just because you were having fun with her and, by the way, gave her my date?"

Then Summer explained to me what happened, which

you already read about but was news to me at the time. So I'm, like, "Oh."

The important thing is that while I was dealing with betrayal issues and Summer was explaining herself, nobody was watching Spike and Scooter.

Jennifer was off talking to Mayor Ed and wasn't watching them, either. But she's used to having boys stand around and wait until she comes back. In fact, poor Randy Frasier was still waiting for her. Summer and I, on the other hand, should have known better. Nobody waits around for us.

So I'm feeling better about the betrayal aspect of the situation and Summer and I decided to not dwell on past issues and go forth from there. In fact, we were kind of teary over it, due in part to our everlasting friendship and in part to "The Long and Winding Road," which The Beatles Experience started after "Twist and Shout."

We hugged each other and promised never to fight again, which we always do at times like that. Thankfully, Summer had Kleenex, and I had lip gloss, so we were able to get ourselves together pretty quickly.

Then, not wanting to waste the emotional rush, we decided to let Spike and Scooter put their muscley fifteen-year-old arms around us and slow dance us until we turned to mush. We turned toward them. "Eeeeek!"

Spike and Scooter were gone!

"Summer!" I said. "We've been ripped off!"

Untransmutation

By that time there were about a thousand people in the Kickapoo Pavilion, plus the lights were turned down because of the slow dance and everything. So there wasn't much use in trying to find them by looking through the crowd. We went straight to the refreshment booths.

"Uh-oh!" we both said at the same time, which would have been cute except for the current circumstances. Every single refreshment booth was out of refreshments. That was significant!

It's not that we thought Spike and Scooter had obliterated the refreshment booths. There was, after all, a couple of hundred boys there between the ages of twelve and fourteen, so the refreshment booth obliteration was unavoidable. It's just that with refreshments gone, there was nothing to interest Spike and Scooter in that regard.

Summer had run out of Ding Dongs a long time ago, although she did get Randy Frasier to stop at the Circle K before they got to the dance and before Jennifer broke up with him. There she loaded up on cookies, but those were gone now, too. Neither one of us had brought the Juicer Gooser.

We started looking through the crowd, hoping that they were dancing. It didn't even matter to us who they were dancing with, because if they weren't dancing, that left only one other thing rats like to do besides running on treadmills and eating.

Spike and Scooter were buff, cute, and fifteen in human years. Me and Summer had created Frankenstein dates!

It was well known that there had been a minor rodent problem in the utility room, so Summer and I were going to look in there first. Jennifer and Mayor Ed were standing in front of the door.

"But I'm Junior Miss Indiana!" Jennifer was saying to Mayor Ed.

"I know, dear," he said, kind of comforting her. "It's just that we have a real television personality in town. I, along with the Better Business Boosters of Glenwood, have to take advantage of this opportunity to boost better business."

"But I'm their Sweetheart," she said as her face flushed and her voice broke a little.

"And always will be until next October, when a new Sweetheart is elected."

Something had happened. It was the thing I had wanted the most since that day in the second grade when Jennifer first got preferred seating on the story rug.

"Don't you worry, we'll still make time to honor you. Right after we honor Mel Ching of The Donut King, who will be after Ms. Savage."

"I'm after The Donut King?" She could barely get it out.

"Well, dear," he began. "The Donut King provided all the paper goods for tonight, not to mention thirty-five-dozen assorted doughnuts. And if there isn't enough time for you this year, we'll make up for it next year. I'm sure you understand." But she didn't understand. Not at all.

For the first time in her life, Jennifer Martin was not going to be honored first, foremost, and only. For the first time in her life, she was going to feel what it was like to be pushed aside in favor of somebody else. It didn't matter how many times she had been Annie or that her brother knew Britney Spears from his days on *The New Mickey Mouse Club.* Jennifer Martin was going to have to take a number and wait, just like the rest of us.

"It's not as bad as you think, Jennifer," said Mayor Ed. "Everyone still loves you." And he gave her a little pat on the head. Summer and I knew that little "there, there" pat on the head. We got it a lot.

We also knew the look on Jennifer's face. It was that pinched-lip smile that tried to say, "Everything is okay," when it was totally not. We heard the squeak in her voice and saw her eyes glisten and we're like, "Man, she's crying over not getting honored at the stupid Spring Fling? How dumb is that?"

Right then I realized that we were so lucky. See, Jennifer was like this little porcelain doll that had to be protected inside a glass case where everything was just the way she needed it to be. She wasn't equipped to live in a world where your brain can get X-rayed or you could lose a kidney.

Summer and I had been toughened up by a world where very strange things happen for no reason and on a daily basis. We thought that, generally speaking, any day that your nose didn't get unexpectedly broken was a good day and had a chance of getting better as it went along.

Right then I started hoping that fate would always be on Jennifer's side because unlike us, she couldn't get through life any other way. It was like, Jennifer was the one who needed the help. Summer and I were okay.

This was such a way better epiphany than the first epiphany I had that day. You know? It was about being a better person and was also accompanied by "The Long and Winding Road," which was so perfect for the moment.

But it turned out that fate was still on Jennifer's side after all. It came blasting through the door in the form of Officer Henderson, who pushed by us going so fast, he almost knocked Summer down.

"Mayor Ed," said Officer Henderson. "Herb the Handyman has taken Regina Leigh Savage hostage!"

"Uh-oh!" we said for about the twelfth time that night.

"He called the station house and said he was holding her until she told him where Doris Trowbridge's body was stashed!"

"Doris who?" asked Mayor Ed.

"We're working on tracing the call."

Summer turned to me and said, "Haven't they ever heard of star sixty-nine?"

"Did you try star sixty-nine?" Mayor Ed asked. And so Officer Henderson talked into his walkie-talkie and said, "Try star sixty-nine." Summer could so be mayor of this town someday.

"Mayor Ed," said Jennifer, now feeling better because fate was back on her side, "because of this startling and highly unusual turn of events, I suggest we go on as originally planned. I get honored first, for winning Junior Miss Indiana. This Regina whatever person can be honored afterward if there's time. And if she survives."

Mayor Ed's smile left for good at the thought of a popular daytime drama star being offed in Glenwood.

And then Mel Ching, The Donut King, and his growing family showed up, carrying boxes of assorted doughnuts. "We brought more doughnuts, Mayor Ed, to replenish the obliterated refreshment booths."

"We are mighty grateful for the doughnuts, Mel," said Mayor Ed as he popped two antacid tablets. "But right now we have a situation on our hands."

"Have you met my son?" said Mel, beaming over a kid who was completely hidden by the doughnut boxes he was holding.

"I didn't even know you had a son," said Mayor Ed.

"Neither did I, but I always wanted one."

"The call was made from old town," said Officer Henderson, snapping off his walkie-talkie and acting like star sixty-nine was his idea. "Hidden Treasures."

"UH-OH!"

Mayor Ed and Officer Henderson walked quickly from the Kickapoo Pavilion and out through the carnival rides, heading toward the parking lot. They didn't want anyone to think that something was wrong and that there was a hostage situation in Glenwood. Summer and I were right behind them, except we were running.

We thought if we got to Hidden Treasures, we could lend credibility to Doris' story, which she must have told Herb the Handyman. Obviously, he was having trouble with it.

"What about Spike and Scooter?" Summer said. Oops. I had forgot all about them.

We turned around and ran back to the dance. Then I stopped.

"We could fix all this if we had the ring!" And Summer goes, "Doris has the ring!" And I go, "Doris lost the ring!" And Summer's, like, *"What?!"*

I forgot to tell Summer that when I got to the dance, but that was because I thought I was betrayed at the time.

So we made another U-turn to go out and start hunting for the ring, which we assumed Doris didn't find because if she had, she would have made herself Doris again and there would be no hostage situation at Hidden Treasures. But we didn't like leaving Spike and Scooter on their own, either.

The truth is, we would have been making U-turns all night except for—"UH-OH!!!" OUR MOMS!

We saw them coming into the carnival area from the parking lot. They were obviously in attack mode and it was so completely unfair! I knew I was going to get busted, but it wasn't supposed to happen until the next day, when my mom saw Mrs. Kochendorfer. Then I remembered that Jennifer went by my house before she got to Summer's. It must have been right after I left. And I'm thinking, Thanks a lot, Jennifer!

"We could tell them the truth," Summer suggested as we

watched them getting closer and closer, looking all around the carnival for us.

"Summer! The 'truth' is what got me grounded in the first place!"

We ran back to the Kickapoo Pavilion but got stopped because we didn't get our hands stamped when we ran out. Lucky for us, the lady with the Susan B. Anthony dollars remembered me and we got back in, but Summer stopped just inside the door.

"Wait a minute!" she said. "Why am I running? I didn't sneak out or anything. Why should *I* be in trouble?"

Summer had forgotten that she lived in Glenwood and how everybody always finds out everything. I explained in as much detail as I could, time permitting.

"Jennifer blabs to my mom about the guys from Sweden. My mom knows something doesn't add up. She goes into my room and finds Raggedy Ann snoring away. She alerts the Mothers of Teenage Girls Telephone Ring of Glenwood. It probably took all of about twenty seconds to hear about us at the mall, Summer."

"Yeah, but why does that make *me* in trouble?" asked Summer. "My mom knew we were at the mall."

"She didn't know a Swedish guy licked you."

"Eeeeek!" Summer grasped the reality of her situation.

It would be harder for them to find us in the dance because of the crowd and the darkness, but they would still find us, sooner or later. I was hoping that for once, the weirdness of life would work in our favor and that something totally weird would save us. But except for two rat boys being loose, and

Mel Ching having a son that he didn't know about, and Rod without Tod, and Heather and Blair without Jennifer, there wasn't anything weird about the dance as far as I knew.

It was clear to me that we had to create our own weirdness. "Okay," I said. "Faint!"

Summer's, like, "What?"

"Faint!" I said. "You have a medical history of doing that and they won't yell at us if you have to be rushed to the emergency room!"

"What happens when I get to the emergency room?" Summer isn't very good with plots.

"You wake up! Everybody's so relieved that you don't have brain damage, we get off with just a lecture."

"But . . ."

"Summer! Faint! Right now and I mean it!" She picked up on the urgency in my voice, looked for a clean spot on the floor, and crumbled. It was pretty dramatic, considering she didn't have time to practice.

"Oh, no!" I cried. "Summer's fainted!"

"What did she do, look in the mirror or something?"

"Hey, was that a remark?" Summer said from the floor.

Heather and Blair had their arms around Spike and Scooter and all four of them were stepping over Summer on their way to the exit.

"Where do you think you're going with our dates?" I said, with understandable outrage.

"What?" Summer said, popping up from her fainted position to see what was going on.

"Your dates?" said Blair in a particularly bratty way. "Well,

your dates want to go out to the parking lot with *us*."

"Blether, Hair . . ." I caught myself. "Sorry, I didn't mean that; I'm just kind of stressed is all." I started again, speaking clearly so they would understand.

"Heather, Blair, these guys are *rats*. Okay?"

"Maybe to you," replied Heather. "But they're nice to us."

"You look so good in pink," said Scooter, to no one in particular.

"It's more like dusty rose," Heather said, referring to what I thought was a pretty frumpy outfit.

"He's talking about me!" said Summer from the floor, indicating her pink *Glam* top.

"HE'S NOT TALKING ABOUT ANYBODY!!!" I screamed.

"Have you seen our all-new Ford Explorer?" asked Spike.

"GOD, YOU HAVE AN EXPLORER?!!!" shrieked the twins together. "That is so cool."

"Spike and Scooter got a car?" asked Summer. And you have to admit that considering everything else, it wasn't that far-fetched.

"No!" I said. "It's just that probably, somewhere in the crowd, Mr. Buckminster of Buckminster Ford was talking to someone about his new car inventory! They hear stuff and add it to their lexicon!"

"What's a lexicon?" asked Blair.

"A glossary or list of words!" said Summer.

"You two are so totally strange," said Blair. "And always have been."

"Oh, yeah!" said Summer, until she could think of something better.

"Bucket," said Scooter.

"Yeah," said Heather, agreeing with Scooter.

I had this serious feeling that everyone was missing the point.

"The point is," I said, "These guys don't mean anything they say! It's just words and that's all! There's only one thing they want out in that parking lot, and it's not food and it's not a treadmill!"

"She is sooo losing it," Heather said to her sister.

"Errr baaag!" said Spike and Scooter as all four of them headed for the exit.

"YOU'RE GONNA LOSE IT," I warned. "IN THE PARKING LOT."

Then, just when everything seemed blackest, weirdness came through for us.

"How come you're on the floor?" asked Rod, almost falling over Summer.

"It wasn't my idea!" she said.

"Oh, no! Summer's fainted!" I cried, remembering the original plan.

"No, she hasn't," said Rod. "She's watching Blair and Heather and those two guys."

"Will you get out of here?!"

Then Summer got up off the floor. "You faint if you want— I'm going to try and find the ring and get us out of this!"

"Like that's going to be so easy!"

"I found a ring," Rod said, trying to butt into a private conversation, which I was glad he did.

"Where?"

"In the gutter."

Kaboing!!! Of course! About half a block from the Foodliner! I should have realized, for crying out loud!

"Except I don't have it anymore."

"WHAT?"

"It was in my room, then it wasn't there anymore."

"Your brother had it in his hand!" I reminded him.

"Know what else I don't have? A brother."

"Stop it, Rod!" It was time to get serious. "There's a hostage situation in old town and another kind of situation in the parking lot! Now where is Tod?"

"Tod who?" said Summer.

"His twin brother!"

"Twin brother?" said Rod.

"Named Tod?" said Summer. "Like, Rod and Tod? That would be pretty weird."

And then this guy walks up to me and goes, "What does KIK 105 do?" And I'm, like, "Please, I'm trying to think. Okay?"

Then I get it! It's, like, *ka-boing* number two.

I broke the news to Rod that, as weird as it sounded, he did have a twin brother. The only reason nobody knew about it was because Tod wished himself into another family because he didn't want to clean up his room!

"Pretty weird, all right," said Summer.

"Even weirder, I think he's Chinese."

It was extremely lucky for us, I might add, that Judy and my mom got delayed at the entrance to the dance. The Correct Change sign was up and they only had large bills. While having to buy cotton candy in order to break a fifty didn't improve their mood, it did give us time to find the Chings.

Because doughnuts were now the only thing at the refreshment booths, the line was very long. Harsh words were exchanged as me, Summer, and Rod cut in at the front.

"That's my twin?" said Rod, looking at the former Tod, whose name was transmutated to Davis Ching and whose ethnic heritage was now Chinese.

"I don't see any resemblance at all," said Summer.

"Look," I said. "This morning Lu Ching told me that she was expecting their first kid. Okay? So unless there's some kind of rapid development thing I missed in biology the week I was out with strep, something's going on! I hope."

Then I turned to the former Tod and asked if he had a small ring anywhere on his person. He thought for a second. He put down a box of assorted doughnuts and reached in his pocket. There was the ring!

"That is so strange," said Summer, who was nonetheless happy. We grabbed the ring, reintroduced Davis to his brother, Rod, and jammed for the door. We didn't get far.

"MARCI KATLIN!!!"

"SUMMER ANN!!!"

Our two totally bent moms had spotted us. They tossed their cotton candy, rolled up their sleeves, and zeroed in on us like laser beams. We panicked.

We both squeezed the ring and wished as fast as we could that everything would untransmutate back to the way it used to be. The list was long, but what I left out, Summer remembered.

Poof.

"That was it?" asked Summer. "A squeaky little *poof*?" It

141

hardly seemed like enough, but we were reassured when we were stabbed with, *"Hey!"* in stereo.

Rod & Tod, together again! Not only that, despite untransmutation, Tod had managed to hang on to two dozen glazed doughnuts, so the whole experience had been worth it as far as they were concerned. We couldn't say the same at that moment.

"Missy!" In my family, being called "missy" is even worse than being called by your first and middle names.

Summer and I whirled around and came face-to-face with our moms. Sensing a nuclear explosion about to happen, Rod & Tod took their doughnuts and split.

Up onstage, The Beatles Experience was taking a break so Jennifer Martin could be honored. And just as she was center stage and in the spotlight, this guy comes up to her and says, "What does KIK one-oh-five do?" And Jennifer goes, "KIK 105 rocks!" And the guy is all like, "Jennifer Martin, you win a trip to Maui!"

How perfect was that? Jennifer goes to Maui and we get dragged off the dance floor and out the exit!

"Mom," I warned. "I am going to have such self-esteem issues later in my life because of this, I can't even tell you." She didn't seem to care that much. She had other things on her mind.

"Who are these boys from Sweden?" she demanded.

"We never said they were from Sweden."

"They're really Russian," said Summer, who thought she was helping.

"Oh, now you change the story!" said Judy. And then she

goes, "What's this I hear about somebody licking you in the food court?"

"It was just my hand, Mom." Summer showed her the hand involved as she added, "I washed it with warm water right after."

"And haven't I told you that pink top is not appropriate?"

"Yes," said Summer, pulling it down and trying to cover her belly button. Then it was my mom's turn.

"And *you*! Just what did you think you were doing by sneaking out like that? Huh?" She doesn't really want me to answer questions like that, but she looks at me like she does.

"Well, I—"

"Don't try and make excuses! Do you know what's in Camden, missy?! Do you?" This question I am supposed to answer.

"Westerly Academy for Girls, where Jane Eyre went to school." I didn't say that last part, but that's the whole point.

"Another stunt like this, and you are on the waiting list!" Then she goes, "In fact, I'm sending for a brochure tomorrow!"

Actually, my grades weren't good enough to get into Westerly, but we both pretended we didn't know that.

Then Heather and Blair came running back from the dance with eyes the size of banjos.

"You know those two Swedish guys?" they said, not noticing the "shut up" looks Summer and I were giving them.

"As soon as we were in the parking lot with them, they turned into rats!"

And my mom goes to us, "See what can happen?"

Short-Term Memory Loss

*A*gain we're being marched, this time from the Kickapoo Pavilion past the Tilt-A-Whirl and right out to the parking lot. Judy had Summer rewashing her hand with a moist towelette, which Judy always carries.

Summer's Voyager was farther down than our Caravan. The last I heard of her on March 22 was, "Call me when you're finished getting punished. Okay?"

"In about twenty years!" my mom answered for me.

I still had the ring and I was trying to figure out some sort of transmutation that would get me out of this. The only thing I could think of was to transmutate my mom into Jennifer Martin's mom, who probably wouldn't care about any of this. But, you know . . . I like my mom sometimes and my dad would notice the difference, anyway.

Then, as we got to our Caravan, I spotted a brand-new

Ford Explorer two slots over. The door was open, like somebody had left in a great big hurry.

"Just a second, Mom?"

"No, in the van! Right now!"

"This will explain everything, I promise!"

I ran to the Explorer and sure enough, Spike and Scooter (in rat form) were up on the door, looking at themselves in the rearview mirror and making little squeak sounds, which was probably rat for, "What happened?"

I picked them up and got into the Caravan. My mom screamed, not seeing how two rats explained anything.

Sometimes I think that if an asteroid fell out of the sky and hit the earth and destroyed everything, the first thing my mom would say would be, "Marci Kornbalm, I better not find out you're responsible for this!"

I talked her into going by Hidden Treasures so I could put Spike and Scooter back in their cage. What I really wanted to do was give the ring back to Doris. Frankly, transmutation hadn't worked out that great for me.

There were police cars all over the place along with the *GLENWOOD: At Six, on Six* cheesy cable news van. As we came to a stop, my mom goes, "Marci Kornbalm, I better not find out you're responsible for this!"

"I'm not, Mom." At least I didn't think I was. In fact, thinking back, there was hardly anything I was responsible for, except sneaking out and telling Jennifer we had dates in the first place. Take those two things away and I was a total victim of circumstance.

"I just gotta put the rats back is all." And I slipped out before she could stop me. The seat belt on her side sticks, so I can usually bail while she's still fooling with it.

I was up to the front door by the time she got out and started yelling at me. The GLENWOOD: At Six, on Six news team assumed she was hysterical over the hostage situation and moved in to videotape her, which slowed her down even more. This was good, because police were blocking the front door and I had to run around the block to the back.

Everyone was in the front part of the shop when I came in the back and put Spike and Scooter in their cage. I heard what was going on and realized that Doris, who was transmutated back into Weird Doris, was still in trouble even though she was no longer Regina Leigh.

From what I could tell, Herb the Handyman had been holding Regina Leigh Savage hostage and telling her how wonderful Doris was and how much he liked her and how he wasn't going to let a popular daytime drama star bump her off and get away with it. Doris probably tried to explain the situation but, after all, how could you explain something like that? Transmutation is a difficult concept.

The police showed up, surrounded the place, and, just about the time Summer and me were wishing everything back the way it was, they broke in through the front door. With everything poofed back to normal, they found Doris instead of Regina Leigh Savage.

Herb the Handyman was looking out the window and didn't actually see the untransmutation happen, thank God. I mean, he already has a significant stuttering problem.

When I slipped in the back door, Mayor Ed was demanding to know where Regina Leigh Savage was, but Doris wasn't listening. She was looking deep into the eyes of Herb the Handyman.

"Did you really mean that, Herb? About how much you liked Doris? I mean, how much you like me, who is Doris?"

"I always did like you, Doris." His stutter got a little worse, but he managed to also say, "I'm very, very happy that you're not murdered."

"Oh, Herb. That's the nicest thing anyone ever said to me," she replied. I would hate to think that was true. Probably she was just encouraging him.

"I don't know what's going on here or why," Mayor Ed said. "What I do know is that I'm missing a popular daytime drama star! You say this all happened because of a ring? Where is it? Let's see it!"

So I'm like trying to figure out someplace to put the stupid ring so Doris would find it and be able to show it to them. I was going to put it in the cage with Spike and Scooter but decided not to. For all I knew, they could transmutate themselves. Heather and Blair had escaped once and it was better not to risk a second time.

"I told you," said Doris. "I lost it."

"Please," said Mayor Ed, "don't give me any of that short-term-memory-loss jazz!"

As I'm putting the ring down on her recliner I go, "I wish they all had short-term memory-loss."

Poof.

"Oops."

See, I still had the ring in my hand when I said that. So I accidentally transmutated everybody's brains. I don't know if it was everywhere or just in Glenwood, but suddenly everything was quiet, like everybody forgot what they were going to say. You know? Then, of course, the cuckoo clocks go off.

So I said to the ring, "Just about junk today, I mean." *Poof.* I tiptoed to the doorway and peeked out into the shop.

Mayor Ed was yelling at Officer Henderson, who couldn't explain why he had dragged the mayor away from the spring fling, so that part was okay. The bad part was Doris and Herb, who had also forgotten that they just had a breakthrough moment in their relationship.

"I guess I'll be going now," said Herb, just like he had ever since they were in high school.

So I quickly grabbed the ring and added, "And not about whatever Doris and the handyman guy were talking about when I came in." I crossed my fingers.

"Or I could stay for a while, if you want, Doris," Herb stuttered.

"I want," Doris said, smiling at him.

"And I was wondering if you would like to go out sometime, too," he said.

And I'm thinking, Golly, this is sooo sudden, Herb. *Not!* But, you know. Better late than never.

I was so totally proud of myself and the way that I had extricated me, Summer, Doris, Rod & Tod, and even Heather and Blair. Except for not going to Maui, and not having dates, things had worked out pretty okay. And it was even okay that we didn't have dates, because Jennifer forgot that I ever said anything about it. *Ta-da!*

My mom had forgotten all about the rat boys from Sweden and about me sneaking out and Summer getting licked, which is good. I hate to see her worry about stuff like that. Of course she wondered about why we had stopped at Hidden Treasures on the way home. I told her it was probably because we saw all the police cars, which was sort of true. As far as the police and news guys go, they were probably very confused. But Summer and I are confused a lot of the time and we know that just because something is confusing doesn't mean it can't be good in some way.

As we pulled into the driveway Mom said, "Marci, I'm trying to remember something about you."

I'm thinking, Uh-oh.

"This morning at breakfast when you asked if you could have your own telephone in your room, what did we say? Yes or no?"

This was an example of something confusing turning out good. Another example was lower basic cable rates, which the city council voted for, even though they forgot why they did.

Summer had forgotten all about everything, just like everybody else in Glenwood, and it took me most of the next morning to explain it to her. She was totally freaking out over the whole thing, especially the part with us in the garage with Spike and Scooter.

I told her about the magic ring not being able to make things appear out of thin air but only being able to transmutate stuff. Summer understood completely.

We grabbed an old globe she had that was no good anymore because it was from before the collapse of the

Soviet Union and ran over to Hidden Treasures, where we planned to use the ring to transmutate it into a digital phone or pager for her (she hadn't decided).

"Lost it?!"

That was us after Doris said she found a ring on her recliner but forgot where she put it. She was talking to a customer and not giving us her totally undivided attention.

"Think, Doris! Please!"

"Girls, I'm helping this lady." Then she goes, "I put it someplace for safekeeping. Go in the back and look if you want." And we did.

"It didn't look like it was worth much," she said to the customer. "But you never know. That will be five dollars, please."

And the customer picked up the little fake gold box and rattled it. "There's something inside," she said. "Do you have the key?"

"No, I don't," said Doris. "Tell you what—make it two-fifty."

When I heard the door open and close, I knew the customer was gone. I said, "Can you help us find it now, please?" Then the phone rang. And instead of helping us look for the ring, she starts yakking with Herb the Handyman. It's like not enough that she sees him every day—she has to talk to him on the phone all the time.

We never did find the ring in Doris' shop that day. Much to her credit, Summer was philosophical about the whole thing. She never once made me feel bad over the fact that I got my own telephone and she didn't.

As for Doris, all I can say is, living with her is pretty difficult these days. Everything is all about her boyfriend and what she should wear. Honestly.

One Year Later

I decided to write this story because I had this assignment in English. "The Most Interesting Thing That Ever Happened to You," ten pages, double-spaced. Perfect, I thought. I get a telephone and also help out my grade in English, which needed helping at the time.

I got a D-plus. How unrewarding was that for such an interesting experience?

The teacher, whose name I shall not mention, and who obviously doesn't like me, said the assignment was to write a *true story.* I told her it *was* a true story. And she goes, "What proof do you have?" Suddenly I'm facing this whole big challenge to my personal integrity!

So I tell her I have my own phone, which my parents told me (in front of witnesses) that I couldn't have and then said I could for no "normal" reason. And I have Spike and Scooter, who now live at my house and seem fairly well adjusted and will do this sort of rat dance if I turn our stereo up loud enough and set them on top of the speakers. Also, the assignment was to write ten pages and I wrote *fifteen*, and everybody knows only something that really happened could be fifteen pages long.

"How much proof do you need, for crying out loud?" I said.

"What did she say?" Summer asked, right after my meeting with the unnamed teacher, which I had to stay after school for and, being the good friend that she is, Summer stayed after and waited for me.

"She also said I lost points for grammar, which she said was hardly recognizable as English."

Summer was shocked that any supposed teacher of English would say something like that. Especially since I had included twelve *Word Wealth* words, not including *transmutation*.

"Not only that," I told Summer. "She said I needed to explain why I was the only one who could remember, and had no short-term memory loss, when everybody else did. And why I knew Rod had a brother when nobody else did."

"That never bothered me," Summer said, and I consider her to be a fairly analytical person.

I said, "Look. Everything in life, practically, is a mystery and nobody's there to explain it to me. How come I gotta start explaining stuff?"

"Good one, Marci," Summer said, getting the point right away.

However, because I desperately needed to raise my grade in English, my teacher gave me a second chance. I could raise the D-plus up to a C if I rewrote the ending.

* * *

So it's like one year after all this happened. My feeling is that the magic ring might still be kicking around Glenwood somewhere. This is because a lot of magic stuff has happened in the last twelve months and things aren't as boring as they used to be.

Both Summer and I got our braces off earlier than expected. Now we have retainers, which are way more cool for obvious reasons, like getting rid of them should the social situation require it. We are really good at it and can slip them out and tuck them into their multicolored designer cases without anyone ever seeing us do it.

Jennifer Martin doesn't eat my brain anymore, not like she used to, which is a pretty big transmutation for me, considering how I've felt about her practically my whole life.

Usually in movies or on TV, like on *Carlton Plaza*, somebody like Jennifer has their own epiphany about things, apologizes for being so obnoxious, and becomes a better person. Either that or they get killed. In real life, that doesn't happen much. You know?

Jennifer's Jennifer and always will be and don't hold your breath waiting for her to apologize for it, or for something bad to happen to her because of it, or for her to learn any kind of lesson in regard to it.

Being too old for *Annie*, she moved on to star in the Indianapolis Musical Theater's production of *Grease*. I can't say one hundred percent that I don't still get a little envious sometimes. When Summer and I saw her in *Grease*, we both wished we had paid a little more attention in Miss Vicky's dance class. But mostly, we're okay with it.

What Summer and I finally figured out is that we are the real Hidden Treasures. And if some people don't know that, it's their problem and not ours. Like Doris said, sometimes you have to look closely to see how wonderful something really is. And I'm not just talking about us here, either.

I have to tell you, the biggest reason why I think the ring might still be around somewhere has to do with Rod & Tod Cort. DORKS NO MORE!

I don't know what happened this year but like, suddenly they'd rather dance than crash into trash cans and they smell like shampoo all the time! How amazingly magical is that?

And they grew a lot, which made Rod perfect for me if I wear heels and Tod perfect for Summer if she doesn't. You know?

This year they picked us up at my house to go to the Spring Fling Dance. They rang the doorbell even, instead of yelling, "Hey!"

Their mom drove and everything, and she looked so relieved to see us in the car with them, and to watch them hold the door for us until we got out, and walk with us instead of running over to see what was in the Dumpster. I'm, like, "Thank you for all of your hard work, Mrs. Cort. Summer and I will take it from here."

So here we are with Rod & Tod, in the Kickapoo Pavilion, and they have the coolest band ever with a singer that's practically Mariah Carey. And they turn the lights down when she sings "Hero." And I look at Summer and she looks at me and we both look at Rod & Tod while our ears are getting all hot and our fingertips start to tingle. And we're all, like, "Put those muscley arms around us, and slow dance us until we turn to mush." And they do.

Spike and Scooter, eat your hearts out.